MW00635112

Scorpia Lives!

Is it possible that the same notorious pirate band that confronted The Phantom four centuries ago has survived into the present day?

When her historical research brings her too close to the truth, Diana Palmer finds herself in deadly peril, and The Phantom moves into action to save his sweetheart and rout his ancient enemy.

Hermes Press

Copyright ©2017 King Features Syndicate, Inc.; ® Hearst Holdings, Inc.; reprinted with permission. All rights reserved.

No part of this book may be reproduced in any form without written permission from the publisher.

Published by Hermes Press, an imprint of Herman and Geer Communications, Inc.
Daniel Herman, Publisher
Louise Geer, Vice President
Troy Musguire, Production Manager
Eileen Sabrina Herman, Managing Editor
Alissa Fisher, Sr. Graphic Designer
Kandice Hartner, Archivist
2100 Wilmington Road
Neshannock, Pennsylvania 16105
(724) 652-0511
www.HermesPress.com; info@hermespress.com

Cover image: Painting of The Phantom by George Wilson
Book design by Eileen Sabrina Herman and Alissa Fisher
First printing, 2017

LCCN 2016942242
ISBN 978-1-61345-122-9
OCR and text editing by H + G Media and Eileen Sabrina Herman
Proof reading by Eileen Sabrina Herman and Margaret Sopkovich

From Dan, Louise, Sabrina, Jacob, Ruk, and Noodle for D'zur and Mellow.

Acknowledgements: This book would not be possible without the help, cooperation, patience, and kindness of many people. First and foremost in making this endeavor a reality are Ita Golzman and Frank Caruso at King Features. Thanks also to Pete Klaus and the late Ed Rhoades of "The Friends of the Phantom." Pete and Ed have provided us with resource material, contacts, information, and helpful insights into the strip and continue to be there when we have questions about the world of The Ghost Who Walks.

Editor's Note: There were several misspellings in the original text; those have been corrected with this reprint. However, the alternate spelling for the Singh pirates as Singg was kept to preserve the original format.

Printed in Canada

THE PHANTOM

**THE PHANTOM and
The Scorpia Menace**

**Lee Falk's original story
adapted by Basil Copper**

CONTENTS

PROLOGUE

How It All Began

*O*ver 400 years ago, a large British merchant ship was attacked by Singg pirates off the remote shores of Bangalla. The captain of the trading vessel was a famous seafarer who, in his youth, had served as cabin boy to Christopher Columbus on his first voyage to discover the New World. With the captain was his son, Kit, a strong young man who idolized his father and hoped to follow him as a seafarer. But the pirate attack was disastrous. In a furious battle, the entire crew of the merchant ship was killed and the ship sank in flames. The sole survivor was young Kit who, as he fell off the burning ship, saw his father killed by a pirate. Kit was washed ashore, half-dead. Friendly pygmies found him and nursed him to health.

One day walking on the beach, he found a dead pirate, dressed in his father's clothes. He realized this was the pirate who had killed his father. Grief-stricken, he waited until vultures had stripped the body clean. Then on the skull of his father's murderer, he swore an oath by firelight as the friendly pygmies watched. "I swear to devote my life to the destruction of piracy, greed, cruelty and injustice, and my sons and their sons shall follow me."

This was the Oath of the Skull that Kit and his descendants would live by. In time, the pygmies led him to their home in Deep Woods in the center of the jungle where he found a large cave with many rocky chambers. The mouth of the cave, a natural formation formed by the water and wind of centuries, was curiously like a skull. This became his home, the Skull cave. He soon adopted a mask and a strange costume. He found that the mystery and fear this inspired helped him in his endless battle against worldwide piracy. For he and his sons who followed became known as the nemesis of pirates everywhere, a mysterious man whose face no one ever saw, whose name no one knew, who worked alone.

As the years passed, he fought injustice wherever he found it. The first Phantom and the sons who followed found their wives in many places. One married a reigning queen, one a princess, one a beautiful red-haired barmaid. But whether queen or commoner, all followed their men back to the Deep Woods, to live the strange but happy life of the wife of the Phantom. And of all the world, only she, wife of the Phantom and their children could see his face.

Generation after generation was born, grew to manhood, assumed the tasks of the father before him. Each wore the mask and costume. Folk of the jungle and the city and sea began to whisper that there was a man who could not die, a Phantom, a Ghost Who Walks. For they thought the Phantom was always the same man. A boy who saw the Phantom would see him again fifty years after; and he seemed the same. And he would tell his son and his grandson; and his son and grandson would see the Phantom fifty years after that. And he would seem the same. So the legend grew. The Man Who Cannot Die. The Ghost Who Walks. The Phantom.

The Phantom did not discourage this belief in his immortality. Always working alone against tremendous—sometimes almost impossible—odds, he found that the awe and fear that the legend inspired was a great help in his endless battle against evil. Only his friends, the pygmies, knew the truth. To compensate for their tiny stature, the pygmies mixed deadly poisons for use on their weapons, in hunting or defending themselves. It was rare that they were forced to defend themselves. Their deadly poisons were known through the jungle, and they and their home. The Deep Woods, were dreaded and avoided. Another reason to stay away from the Deep Woods—it soon became known that this was a home of the Phantom, and none wished to trespass.

Through the ages, the Phantoms created several more homes or hideouts in various parts of the world. Near the Deep Woods was the Isle of Eden, where the Phantom taught all animals to live in peace. In the southwest desert of the New World, the Phantoms created an eyrie on a high sheer mesa that was thought by the Indians to be haunted by evil spirits and became known as "Walker's Table"—for The Ghost Who Walks. In Europe, deep in the crumbling cellars of an ancient castle ruins, the Phantom had another hideout from which to strike against evildoers.

But the skull cave in the quiet of the Deep Woods *remained the true home of the Phantom. Here, in a rocky chamber, he kept his chronicles, written records of all his adventures. Phantom after Phantom faithfully wrote their experiences in the large folio volumes. Another chamber contained the costumes of all the generations of Phantoms. Other chambers contained the vast treasures of the Phantom acquired over centuries, used only in the endless battle against evil.*

Thus, twenty generations of Phantoms lived, fought and died, usually violently, as they followed their oath. Jungle folk, sea folk, and city folk believed him the same man, the Man Who Cannot Die. Only the pygmies knew that always, a day would come when their great friend would lie dying. Then, alone, a strong young son would carry his father to the burial crypt of his ancestors where all Phantoms rested. As the pygmies waited outside, the young man would emerge from the cave, wearing the mask, the costume and the skull ring of the Phantom; his carefree happy days as the Phantom's son were over. And the pygmies would chant their age-old chant, "The Phantom is dead. Long live the Phantom."

In this story, the Phantom of our own time—the twenty-first generation of his line—confronts an evil force that had menaced his ancestor four hundred years ago. This time, the threat strikes close to home, as the Phantom's sweetheart—the beautiful and world-famous American Olympic athlete, Diana Palmer—falls into the clutches of Scorpia.

Lee Falk
New York 1972

CHAPTER 1

The Deep Woods

The brilliant shafts of sunlight, beating down through the fronds of broad-leaved vegetation, sent steam rising from the depths of the Bangalla Jungle. It was already mid-morning and the forest was a-chatter with the screams of brightly-hued birds and the fierce shrieking of monkeys, which swung excitedly from branch to branch. The vivid stripes of the lordly tiger showed momentarily, the muscles undulating beneath the silken skin, as the great beast passed through the glade on his way to a hidden pool to drink.

Somewhere a kakar barked and a herd of deer, grazing in a clearing, lifted their delicate heads in brief alarm, before sinking them to browse again. Even beneath the green umbrella of the jungle and between the boles of great trees, the heat was stifling. The sun brought with it the flickering breath of a furnace, a fiery reminder of the great desert which fringed the jungle not far away.

The sun was life to the people of the desert cities and to the folk of the jungle, but it could also bring death from thirst and torturing heat if not treated with respect. The sun was as much one of the vital factors of the Bangalla Jungle as the lordly tiger himself or the dreaded viper of the deep forest. Now, as its rays struck sharp spears of light through the gloom, a baboon shrieked with sudden fear and bounded upward into the branches of a tree, sending a flock of parrots exploding in a rain of multicolored feathers.

The baboon's alarm was caused by the faint, almost imperceptible passage of hoofs in the soft debris of the jungle floor. Then, from the green of the undergrowth, emerged a huge white horse, walking slowly as it picked its way delicately through the tangled mass of branches and vines. The rider of the white horse reined in and glanced about him keenly, noting the baboon's presence in the tree and seeming to sniff the air like the animals, as if alert to danger.

This big man, who sat his finely-matched mount like a king, was an extraordinary sight. His chunky form was over six feet in height. His face was craggy, broad and good looking. Strong, square white teeth flashed in his tanned features as his eyes ranged the terrain before him. His eyes themselves were covered with a small black mask and his massive torso with a close-fitting jerkin of thin material under which his pectoral muscles stood out sharply.

The iron-hard muscles of his upper arms rippled under the light-colored material whenever he moved. The jerkin was in one piece and rose to a close-fitting hood which held tight to his head so that it was impossible to see the colour of his hair.

His legs and thighs were encased in similar material and his feet in thick black riding boots. He wore two revolvers in black leather holsters at either side of his body. Around his middle he wore close-fitting shorts of a thick striped cloth and over that a massive black belt. On the front of this was a triangular motif which had a tiny skull-symbol in the center. The effect should have been bizarre and sinister but it wasn't.

This was The Phantom, the man superstition whispered could never die; of whom a thousand legends were circulated over as many miles of jungle. The spirit of the Deep Woods of the Bangalla Jungle, a man of tradition, a god almost, whose life was dedicated to overthrowing evil. Men said he had lived for hundreds of years; that he could never be killed and the sight of him in this wild and remote place would have convinced any watcher that the legends were true, so durable and eternal did he look, sitting at ease on the white horse's back as though carved of bronze.

Nothing moved except The Phantom's eyes as he surveyed the terrain; the group formed by the man and the horse was like a statue, so perfect was the rapport between master and mount. Then The Phantom relaxed. He chuckled, his white teeth showing square and strong in the dim light of the jungle, as he leaned forward to pat the horse's mane. The great stallion whinnied and tossed his head in a lordly gesture at the familiar touch.

"Well, Hero," said The Phantom in a deep, sonorous voice, "We shall be home in another hour."

His booted heels delicately touched Hero's flanks and the

white horse started off again. Hero hardly needed his master's subtly indicated instructions, so much in accord were the two. The character of the forest was now changing slightly, the undergrowth thinning out, with here and there rocky outcrops and once a stream tumbling over boulders into a sparkling pool. The trees too were bigger, their boles more broadly spaced so that The Phantom and his white horse seemed to be within the dim, misty confines of a cathedral.

Then the floor of the jungle rose into a low cliff and through the thick tangle of trees could be seen the white tumble of a descending waterfall. Hero, without hesitation, plunged into the last belt of trees and they came out onto a broad, reed-fringed pool into which the waterfall descended with a loud roar, the water foaming white where the spray mingled with the sunlight to form rainbows.

Hero splashed hock-deep into the pool and made straight for the cliff face over which the waterfall tumbled with a dizzy tumult. The water made a brilliant white, dazzling wall through which it seemed impossible to penetrate. But The Phantom and Hero went imperturbably on, the horse needing no urging from his master, he had repeated the process so many times.

Then they were within the heart of the torrent, the shock of the descending water in its drenching cascade blotting out the sunlight, the roar of the fall drumming in their ears and making them momentarily deaf. But Hero kept on placing his feet with great deliberation and precision and a few seconds later brilliant sunlight dazzled their eyes. Then they were through, The Phantom wiping his streaming eyes, Hero shaking his head impatiently to clear the droplets. Steam rose in shimmering clouds from man and horse as the heat of the sun smote them like a sword-stroke. Hero splashed through another shallow pool and then they were on firm ground, safe within a secret valley, known only to The Phantom and a few jungle folk, including the Bandar pygmy tribe.

Around them towered tall cliffs, clothed with densely-packed vegetation. Within this narrow and fertile valley The Phantom had his headquarters and carried on his implacable war against crime and injustice wherever it reared its head. Presently, Hero and The Phantom had passed up the valley and the great white horse quickened its steps as it sensed they were nearing home. The sun had already long dried them when they came in sight of one of the most amazing sights of the Bangalla Jungle, itself an incredible place.

Here were the Deep Woods, The Phantom's secret home, where he planned his ceaseless war against organized crime and the only place where he was able to relax his ceaseless vigilance. So he let the reins slacken on Hero's neck as they drew near to home and allowed himself to day-dream a little of a dark-haired girl who was now many thousands of miles away.

Hero's hoofs clattered across rock, striking sparks from the unyielding surface, startling The Phantom from his brief reverie. Across the rocky valley was the familiar clearing. Set in the cliff-face opposite and brightly delineated in the sunshine loomed a massive formation which gave The Phantom his feared motif and which he had seen a hundred times before on returning from long and perilous journeys.

From the cliff-face, created by the natural formation of the tumbled stone, stared the representation of a massive skull. The skull itself was all of eighty feet high. Two large caves in the crumbling cliff above made gigantic eye-sockets; below, a fall of rock in some earlier time had left a ruined gash which looked uncannily like the remains of the nose; the gigantic entrance below, black within, slashed with bars of sunlight without, made an enormous, open mouth. The cave entrance was all of thirty feet high and Hero's hoofs echoed eerily beneath the roof as he clattered into the tunnel, The Phantom swinging to dismount as they gained the interior.

The rough stone walls twisted for some distance and then broadened out into a great chamber. Torches burned flickeringly in wall sockets, casting a strange, uneven light over the surface of the cave interior. The Phantom rapidly unsaddled Hero and set him out to forage. As the stallion's hoofbeats died away beyond the arch of the tunnel The Phantom sank with satisfaction onto a great pile of skins at one side of the chamber. Here, where a natural formation of the floor had assumed the semblance of a couch, he made his bed. He unbuckled his pistol-belt and stretched his legs in their black riding boots. The flickering torches left the far side of the cave in shadow. The Phantom grunted. He went over to his saddle bags and busied himself with the provisions they contained. He crossed to the far side and blew the ashes of the fire in the rough stone hearth into flame. For the next half-hour he was engrossed in preparing his midday meal.

When it was ready he carried the platters to his couch of skins and sat. He ate with satisfaction, his thoughts far away from his primitive surroundings. He was still sitting there lost in contemplation when he became aware of a faint, furtive footstep in the tunnel outside.

"Come in, Guran," The Phantom called in a loud, amused voice. The footsteps stopped, as though the owner of the feet which had made them was frightened. Then they came on again, less hesitantly this time. A diminutive figure eased forward into the fitful light of the torches. The torch-flicker glinted on small, yellow eyes as the tiny brown man bowed in deference to The Phantom who, sprawled on his couch of skins, regarded him with an amused smile.

"Welcome, O Ghost Who Walks," said Guran in the dialect of the Bangalla Jungle tribes. "I trust you have had a fruitful and auspicious journey."

"Fruitful, yes," said The Phantom. Humor glinted in his eyes.

"Auspicious, perhaps. I settled two tax disputes and prevented a minor war between the border tribes. Now, I am a little tired and will rest a day or two."

"Perhaps you will join us in hunting?" said Guran.

The little man's face was alight with pleasure as he came forward and stood in the glow given out by the fire.

"Perhaps," said The Phantom smiling. "I really have not yet decided my program. But hunting is a possibility."

There was a suspicion of a smile on the little brown man's face also. Looking at the diminutive form of the chief of the pygmies, clad only in a loin cloth and with his wrinkled feet and tattered straw headgear, The Phantom felt the strange contrast between this mild little man and his fearsome reputation. For the Bandar, with their poison weapons, were among the most feared of the jungle tribes and their activities in the Deep Woods were among the things which helped to keep The Phantom's domains inviolate while he was away from home.

There was a whimpering cry in the tunnel, and the grey form of Devil the mountain wolf and The Phantom's special pet bounded forward in greeting. Guran scuttled to one side of the cave as The Phantom, grinning, fondled Devil's ears. The big wolf's yellow eyes glowed as though with inward fires, and his red tongue lolled over his white, razor- sharp teeth as his master continued his affectionate scratching.

"Has he been good while I've been gone?" The Phantom asked, smiling again as Guran continued to cower, his anxious eyes never leaving the wolf's form.

"Truly, I do not know, O Ghost Who Walks," the pygmy chief answered. "The grey one has his own ways and beware the pygmy who interferes with his arrangements."

The Phantom's laugh echoed through the chamber. He fondled Devil again and then got up. Devil padded at his heels and Guran followed behind as he walked to the cave entrance. Here, to one side of the massive grotto, was The Phantom's lofty throne, where he sat to receive homage from the jungle folk. The big man settled himself in the great carved stone chair and gazed pensively out across the valley. It was already late afternoon and the sun was declining behind the distant trees.

Devil went to sit alongside The Phantom on one of the steps of the massive stone plinth which supported the throne and Guran squatted at the foot of the steps. His brown face, as always, was expressionless, as he gazed fixedly at The Phantom. There was silence among the group for a long time. Once Devil gave a stifled yawn, but the only other sound which broke the silence was the sighing of the wind in the treetops.

The little man was the first to stir. He cleared his throat apologetically and scratched his left foot with the big toe of the right.

"Your thoughts are not with us here in the forest, O Great One," he said gently.

The Phantom dropped his hand to fondle Devil's ears again as the big wolf huddled in closer to the foot of the throne. He smiled as he glanced at Guran.

"You are right, Guran," he said pensively. "My thoughts are many thousands of miles away."

The pygmy chief shifted his position on the hard stone of the steps.

"Would the Great One think it impertinent if Guran were to guess the reason?" he asked.

The Phantom's eyes were sparkling with humor, as he replied.

"It would not, O Great Chief of the Bandar," he said gravely, in his turn.

Guran cleared his throat once more and lifted his gaze to the rim of the distant trees, which were now stained gold with the dying sun.

"I guess, O Ghost Who Walks, that you dream of the fair Diana," he said diffidently. There was a long pause between the two men. Devil shook his head and looked expectantly at the big man seated on the throne as though he understood the conversation.

The Phantom nodded his head.

"Well," he said slowly. "You have a point there, Guran. I must confess my mind has been far away the last day or so. On a long ride one has time to think."

The little man blinked. His eyes glowed with pleasure at the correctness of his suppositions.

He stretched his cramped limbs gratefully as The Phantom got up. Devil stretched too and walked behind as The Phantom strolled down the rocky path leading from Skull Cave with Guran.

The pygmy shot a sidelong glance at The Phantom as he said, "Have you ever thought of marriage?"

The Phantom smiled wistfully. His face was stained scarlet with the sunset and his eyes gleamed behind the mask.

"Constantly, Guran," he said.

He looked round the wild and savage landscape in which they walked.

"But how? To bring a modern girl here to live in a cave? It would be impossible."

Guran made a little shrugging movement of his shoulders, accompanying it at the same time with an expressive wave of his hand and wrist.

"Maybe she thinks differently," he said simply. "Did you ever ask her?"

The Phantom frowned. Then his big face broke up in a slow smile.

"You'd better stick to your witch-doctoring, Guran," he said. "You're far better at it than trying to act as a marriage counselor."

Guran smiled shyly. He went to sit on the trunk of a fallen tree at the side of the track. The Phantom settled by his side as Devil went foraging in the undergrowth. He bounded away after some small animal.

Both men were silent again for a while. The Phantom's mind was heavy with thoughts about Diana. Guran was right. She was the ideal companion for him. Diana Palmer. He and Diana had been friends since childhood when, as Kit Walker, he had been educated in the United States. But it was not until their time at Harrison U. that they had fallen in love.

Diana was a beautiful, dark-haired girl who excelled in all forms of sports. She was proficient at riding and tennis and had hundreds of hours as a pilot. Swimming was a particular specialty and she had won a Gold Medal for diving at the Olympic Games.

He remembered her, poised in her swimsuit at the tip of the diving board; and in his arms as they danced at the Junior Prom before they had fallen in love. All his earliest dreams were intertwined with those of Diana. There had been an emptiness in his life since stern duty brought him back to the Bangalla Jungle to carry on the work entrusted to him by his father.

He and Diana had written often, of course, but symbols on a piece of paper were a pale substitute for the reality of warm, living flesh and the vital personality that made Diana unique among women. He remembered too, the black night when Guran had come for him, to tell him his father was dying. It meant that he and Diana had to part, peremptorily and agonizingly, with only one brief talk and a hurried explanation. It all seemed a long time ago and so much had happened since.

The Phantom's strong face had softened with remembered emotion as he sat on the fallen log, Guran silent at his side. Devil came back suddenly, growling excitedly and rummaging in the bushes. The spell was abruptly broken.

"You will think about it, O Great One?" said Guran encouragingly.

The Phantom stirred and turned to face the little chief of the Banda.

"I'll think about it," he promised.

"It may well come to pass," Guran said.

The Phantom's eyes were again fixed on the farthest jungle trees whose tips were still colored by the dying light of the sun.

"Who knows, Guran, who knows?" he replied.

CHAPTER 2

Olympic Champion

Eleven thousand miles away in Westchester, U.S.A., a tall dark-haired girl was walking along the sidewalk, a bundle of books under her arm. The air was full of the perfume of flowers and the green of the chestnut trees made a rich backing to the trim, shaven lawns that stretched down to the boulevard on either side. But the girl was oblivious to all of these things or to the greetings of the young men who passed her at intervals on the sidewalk.

She returned their sallies in a half-hearted way, barely conscious of what they were saying. Her trim, athletic body with its springy stride was the target of most male eyes as she passed. She wore a blue, open-neck shirt so severe as to be like a boy's and her tailored tartan skirt perfectly molded a form that owed nothing to artifice. Her high, tip-tilted bust strained forward against the blue shirt and a silver medallion on a silver cord round her neck quivered with the motion of her body.

Presently, she turned in through a large, wrought-iron gateway and went up a red gravelled driveway to a white house built in Colonial style. The colonnaded porch and the shutters at the windows proclaimed the influence of the South, but the yellow painted garage that would hold four cars and the kidney-shaped swimming pool on the patio spoke of the comforts of the East.

The girl turned the bronze handle on the big mahogany front

door and went through into a large hall that was gracious with well-waxed antique furniture and bowls of cut flowers that stood about on chests and table surfaces and gave off a pungent perfume in the cool dimness of the interior. She turned into a long room where mellow light shining from outside stenciled the shadows of the French windows across the carpet.

"Is that you, Diana?"

It was a woman's voice; soft and well-modulated. Diana smiled gently at its well-remembered tones and the often repeated question.

"Yes, Mother," she said. "I'm in the drawing room."

The woman whose lithe step sounded in the hall a few moments later showed the remains of great beauty on her face. Though in her late forties she was still elegant and her trim figure had often been mistaken for that of her daughter. Diana moved quickly to greet her mother with an affectionate kiss on the cheek. They were tremendous friends, despite the age-gap, and they always confided in one another.

Mrs. Palmer's hair showed traces of grey now and as she despised cosmetic aids to beauty, she made no effort to tint it as was the modern fashion. She was dressed smartly and expensively in a tailored suit with velvet cuffs and collar that set off her figure to perfection and the basket full of cut sterns in one hand and the clippers in the other showed that she had been engaged in her favorite occupation, cutting and arranging flowers in the elegant rooms of the Palmer home.

Mrs. Palmer paused and put the basket down on a nearby table and then put the clippers in the basket. She dusted her already immaculate hands as though the work of flower arranging had left traces of some soiling physical labor. She looked inquiringly at her daughter who had gone to sprawl on a large, overstuffed sofa, one of her long, elegant legs dangling over the arm.

"Have you enrolled for that course, Diana?"

"Funny you should ask, Mother," Diana said. "I've just been down to register at college. Luckily, there was a vacancy or I wouldn't have got in until the fall. As it is, I start night classes this evening."

Mrs. Palmer smiled with pleasure.

"That is good news, dear, though why you want further qualifications with all your talents I don't know."

Diana frowned. Even that could not disturb the beauty of her face.

"You know I must keep busy, Mother," she said. "I feel the need to do something with my time."

"You've been unsettled ever since Kit Walker left," Mrs. Palmer continued. "He was the one, wasn't he?"

Diana flushed. She shifted her position on the sofa and put her right leg up to join the left.

"That's a leading question, Mama," she said.

Mrs. Palmer smiled again.

"You never did like direct questions on intimate matters, dear," she said. "Your late father was just the same. It must be an inherited trait. But I wouldn't mind betting anything that I'm right."

It was Diana's turn to smile.

"In that case, Mother, you won't need any answer from me," she said. "Anyway, most of the young men around here bore me. All they can talk about when they ask me out to dinner is baseball or the latest figures on the Dow Jones Index."

Mrs. Palmer shot Diane a penetrating glance.

"All the same, dear," she observed. "You have turned down some very eligible young men in the last year or so. It is time you were thinking about marriage."

Diana closed her eyes and lay back with her head against the cushions of the sofa.

"No doubt you're right, Mama," she said. "I sometimes wonder myself why I haven't married."

"There you are, you see," said her mother, as though she had just uttered a profound truth.

"Still, perhaps you'll run across somebody interesting during this new course. What are you taking?"

"Medieval history," Diana said brightly.

Mrs. Palmer frowned.

"Well, no doubt you know best, dear," she said. "Though I must say it does seem a little arid to me."

She looked helplessly round the immaculate drawing room, as though there were hundreds of bowls of flowers that still needed arranging.

"Why not have a swim before dinner, darling? There's plenty of time and the sun's still hot."

Ten minutes later the trim form of Diana, taut and bronzed in her bikini, trotted out onto the lawn at the rear of the house, a Sealyham terrier yapping excitedly behind her. A Japanese gardener hacking away at the roots of a fruit tree in a neighboring garden almost turned a somersault as he caught sight of her. Diana climbed to the top of the diving board, her feet hardly seeming to touch the rungs of the ladder. Then she jack-knifed down from the twenty-foot level. Her arrowed body hit the water so perfectly that she entered the pool almost without a ripple. Something seemed to pull her body down through the water with a minimum of disturbance.

She took an almost sensuous pleasure in swimming and she floated lazily beneath the surface, her hands spread out stiffly above her head, her skin tingling from the freshness of the water, as she drifted to the end of the pool. Then she surfaced, shaking her long, dark hair, conscious of a faint echo of applause. She looked up to see the laughing, boyish face of a trim-looking man in his forties. His blond hair was cut short and a briar pipe was stuck between his square, white teeth. His square jaw re-echoed the theme and he belched furiously at the pipe, which gave off sparks and blue smoke as he continued to applaud.

"Beautiful, Diana," he said.

"Thank you, Uncle David," she said. "I didn't expect you home so early."

"Flew in two hours ahead of schedule," her uncle said. "They had an early warning of electrical storms so I decided not to take the later plane."

He sat down on a rustic bench near the edge of the pool as Diana stroked her way effortlessly through the water.

He knocked the pipe on the wooden arm of the bench, sending a shower of sparks and ash over the tiles.

"Lily tells me you're going to take a night course in medieval history," he said.

Diana shook the water from her hair and gripped the ladder at the side of the pool. She smiled up at David on the terrace.

"It wouldn't have anything to do with Kit Walker, would it?" her uncle grinned. "I remember he came from a long line of buccaneers or something, wasn't it?"

Diana felt herself flushing again.

"Really, Uncle David," she said. "It was sea-captains and admirals and people like that. Pirates, indeed!"

Her uncle smiled again.

"It's a thin division," he said. "Especially when one gets a little farther back in history."

Diana had ducked back beneath the surface of the water again. But later when she went up to change for dinner, Uncle David's words came again to her mind. Kit Walker had been much in her thoughts of late.

CHAPTER 3

Pirate Gold

Diana Palmer ran lightly up the double flight of steps in front of Westchester College as leaves whirled about her in the night wind. Ahead of her the long rows of windows cast yellow beams of light across the campus. She avoided chattering groups of students and made instead for a secluded side door. More and more, Diana was isolating herself from people, working out some of the complex problems of her life in her head. And more and more the smiling face of Kit Walker had crystallized itself into a permanent image in her mind.

Now she made her way down the corridor by a route that avoided the mainstream of student chatter into the library where the Medieval History Class was assembling. There were only a dozen taking part and of these only three were known to Diana personally. However, she nodded pleasantly to the others and settled herself at the desk.

She had already selected the volumes she intended studying and now she assembled the material on the surface of the desk before her. The library was a light and airy place, the ranks of books in teak bookcases making a blaze of color round the walls, and an old pine farmhouse-type clock ticked melodiously on as the minutes passed. Amanda Welch, the dynamic, blonde-haired history teacher in her mid-forties, was already sitting in her famous steel and leather armchair on a dais in front of the students, ticking off something in a leather-covered book.

Now she got up and extended a welcome to the class. Then she went round the tables individually, greeting the students and asking and answering questions. She hesitated momentarily as she reached Diana.

"I noticed your name on the register," she said. "Aren't you Diana Palmer, the Olympic diver and explorer?"

Diana smiled.

"That is true. Miss Welch," she replied, "but I think my achievements have been somewhat exaggerated by the press."

Miss Welch's eyes were sparkling as she gazed at Diana with approval.

"I think you may safely let the public be the judge of that," she said.

"I was rather surprised at your enrolling for this course, that's all." Diana looked puzzled for a moment

"I don't quite follow you, Miss Welch," she said.

Miss Welch tested the pliability of a pencil between her delicately manicured fingers as she gazed across the room at the other students.

"What I'm trying to say, Miss Palmer," she said, "is that this history course must seem pretty tame to you after your travels and all your other accomplishments."

Diana's face cleared. She laughed softly.

"Oh, I see. No, I find it exciting. I think if you put everything into the task of the moment you invariably get something out of it in return. At least, that's what I feel."

Miss Welch's eyes met hers gravely.

"That's a refreshing attitude these days, Miss Palmer," she said ruefully. "I only wish some of our less mature students would take the same attitude."

Diana smiled again.

"Ah, student lib. That's a big question," she said.

"Too big to go into tonight," said Miss Welch. "Particularly during history class."

She tightened her grip on the pencil and tapped it against pink finger nails.

"Forgive me for being personal in saying this," she murmured.

Diana looked at her inquiringly.

"Go ahead," she said.

Miss Welch hesitated. She shifted awkwardly from one foot to the other.

"Well, it's just that one is surprised," she said.

"Surprised about what?" said Diana.

Miss Welch came to the point.

"I wonder why a beautiful and talented girl like you isn't married," she said.

There was a faint flush on her cheeks which had not escaped Diana's notice and which saved her from embarrassment in turn.

"There are reasons, Miss Welch," she said. "Your question was not at all impertinent. I may tell you something more about it when we get to know each another better."

With that Miss Welch had to be content. She turned away to begin her opening remarks. But Diana, head bent down toward her books was already mentally re-echoing Miss Welch's questions. The image of Kit Walker as she had last seen him kept coming between her and the printed pages. Miss Welch was a remarkably shrewd woman. She looked at her now as she sat in her swivel chair, poised and perfectly at ease as she put major historical questions into the context of the course.

Several weeks passed and Diana gradually became absorbed in the course. Under Miss Welch's expert instruction she and the other members of the class made rapid progress and she found history, up until now somewhat dry, an absorbing subject. She had chosen to discuss in a term paper certain characteristics of the sixteenth century and as her researches deepened she found herself concentrating less on the broad aspects of political and trade policies than on the more obscure manifestations of lawlessness in a particularly lawless period.

Diana ransacked the library shelves in her search for little-known, obscure works, and she even sent to the State Archive Offices for sixteenth century journals, newspapers and trade reports that spoke of piracy on the high seas. In her research one name recurred again and again. This was a reference to a band known as the Scorpia.

At first they were mentioned as legends but then as documentation became less scanty, they began to emerge as a well-trained body of lawless adventurers who pillaged honest merchant ships in the early fifteen hundreds. They were encountered on the Spanish main, in the West Indies and even off the coast of Africa. Diana's pencilled notes assumed sizeable proportions and as her studies gained in depth and scope, the activities of the Scorpia gradually became the entire topic of her thesis.

One entry caused her heart to pump faster when she came across it. A report by an agent of Governor Wicks of Jamaica spoke of the Scorpia pirate band in the seventeenth century and said that they had been destroyed by the legendary Phantom. Diana's hand faltered with surprise and she put the book down on the desk. She felt slightly giddy and her heart seemed to be beating with unaccustomed vigor. She looked at the photostat entry of the ancient, faded writing again.

There was no possible doubt about it. It said "The Phantom" clearly enough. The date of the disbandment of the Scorpia band was given as 1612. Diana was master of herself again now. She was conscious that Miss Welch was at her elbow.

"You're still concentrating on the Scorpia, I see, Diana," the teacher said, a faint smile on her face. "I cannot quite understand why you have chosen such a bizarre topic. After all, an unknown pirate band of the seventeenth century will hardly generate much excitement . . ."

She broke off as Diana looked up, interrupting her with a flow of words.

"I can't imagine a more exciting topic, Miss Welch," the girl said. "You see, The Phantom destroyed the band in 1612."

She paused and then went on.

"I put that badly, Miss Welch. I mean The Phantom's ancestor. Not my Phantom."

She stopped, conscious that Miss Welch was staring at her with incredulity in her eyes.

"Your Phantom, Diana?" she stammered. "I'm not at all sure I know what you mean."

"No, as I said, I put it badly," Diana replied. "I'm getting so absorbed in the subject of the Scorpia, I hardly know what I'm saying tonight. It's all so interesting and it's fascinating digging up all the little pieces of information from so many different sources."

Miss Welch smiled again.

"Oh, well, Diana, if you put it like that," she said. "But I wouldn't overwork if I were you. The thesis isn't so important."

"I won't, Miss Welch," Diana said, relaxing. She got up with the others as the session came to an end, and gathered up the books. She would have to guard her tongue a little more carefully. She knew that Kit would not approve of her talking of such secret matters to an outsider. But the subject had not stopped nagging at her mind and when she arrived home she went straight to the big drawing room where she spread out the books again on a table near the window.

It was here Mrs. Palmer found her at two a.m., a steaming mug of coffee at her elbow, when she came down to investigate the light streaming out across the lawn.

"Really, Diana," she said crossly. "You shouldn't keep these hours. You'll never be up in the morning."

She crossed over to the table and picked up one of the books.

"Still this Scorpia business. Don't you get enough of this at night classes?"

"Sorry, Mama," Diana said. Her eyes were bright with excitement and she was completely oblivious of the hour.

"I'll be coming up soon."

"Just make sure you do," said her mother in a stern voice. Then her expression softened and she bent to plant a kiss on her daughter's forehead.

"Just drink the coffee and then up to bed!"

"Sure," said Diana grinning.

She waited until she heard her mother's door close and then went back to her records. She had found that the Scorpia had been only partially destroyed in 1612, even though The Phantom, the band's traditional enemy, had killed the Scorpia leader, Bruned de Gottschalk. He then blew up the powder magazine of the band's castle, obliterating their stronghold.

The writer of the chronicle, who was not named, concluded, "The story is pure legend and there is no historical evidence that the entity called The Phantom ever really lived. But the blackened stones of the castle remain."

Diana put the book down and cupped her chin on her hands. She smiled gently to herself, her imagination once again picturing the scene. Only instead of The Phantom of the ancient chronicle, Kit Walker's strong, square features were superimposed on those imagined by the seventeenth century historian.

"How little they know," she breathed to herself. "That Phantom was an ancestor of my Phantom."

She read on. She had already discovered that the band was only partially destroyed and that the organization had reappeared in the early eighteenth century in East Africa. Later records spoke of the pirates near Suez as late as 1818. Incredibly, the last reference Diana could find, spoke of the China coast in 1898.

She finished the last of the coffee and closed the books.

"That wasn't so very long ago," she told herself.

She frowned.

"Curious. I understood the band had died out."

She got up and went to the window. All was silent, apart from the night wind tapping at the blinds. Diana's eyes saw nothing of the faint lights from the boulevards, stippling the patterns of leaves across the lawn in front of her. Instead, she saw blue water suddenly stained red, the flash of cutlasses, the sprawl of sweating bodies across tilting decks; heard the clash of steel on steel, the screams and groans of the wounded, the sullen roar of cannon.

She shivered suddenly as though the night were cold. Then she went back to the table and cleared her things. She was a long time falling asleep.

CHAPTER 4

Otto Koch is Curious

.

The doorbell rang shrilly as Diana was sitting at breakfast the next day. Her mother came in a few minutes later. Her eyes were bright and mischievous.

"You're famous again, Diana," she said satirically. "Dinah Mulvaney is waiting to interview you in the drawing room."

David Palmer froze in mid-stroke as he was about to decapitate a boiled egg.

"Whoever she may be," he said.

"Don't you ever keep up to date with local news, Uncle David?" said Diana, getting up from the table.

"She's a power in the community. Social Editor of the *Westchester Gazette*, no less."

Uncle David made an expressive movement of his shoulders. He tried hard to put an awed look on his face but failed miserably. Diana and her mother burst out laughing. In fact, Diana had a job composing her face when she opened the double doors to the drawing room a few moments later.

A smartly groomed woman in her thirties, dressed in a tailored suit and a fur wrap got up from a couch to greet her effusively.

"I hear you've taken up night school, Diana," she said approvingly. "I thought we might run a few lines."

She looked at the girl curiously.

"It's certainly original. What made you do it?"

"Do sit down, Miss Mulvaney," her hostess said, leading the way back to the couch.

"It hardly seems important enough to justify even a few lines," she said deprecatingly.

You let us be the judge of that, Diana," said the columnist, getting out a small gold pencil and a miniature pad from her alligator handbag. "Whatever you do is news, my dear. Now what did you say you were studying?"

"I didn't," said Diana mischievously. "But if you must know, it's history and I've chosen to study an obscure pirate band called the Scorpia."

Dinah Mulvaney's pencil remained poised over the paper for just a fraction of a second. Her eyes looked blank. Then her face broke up in a smile.

"Oh, how fascinating," she said. "Our readers will love to hear all about that."

A hard-faced man wearing an expensive blue-striped suit and Palm Beach hat pulled the Fleetwood Cadillac into the curb and sounded the horn peremptorily. The wizened cripple who ran the news-stand hurried eagerly to the window.

"What'll it be, Mr. Cringle?" he asked.

"Sports edition and the *Gazette*," said the man called Cringle. He had cold blue eyes that seemed to look right through the little news-stand proprietor. His long blond hair fell in soft waves beneath the brim of his hat. A faint scar puckered the skin of one bronzed cheek and pulled the lid of his right eye slightly to one side. It gave him a strange and sinister appearance and commanded attention when he spoke.

The little man was back, thrusting the papers through the window.

"Keep the change," said Cringle curtly.

He wound up the window so fiercely he almost caught the newsman's hands. He drove a little farther down the block. A middle-aged man driving a yellow Chevy was trying to park in the one slot available. He was doing a bad job of it. When he had backed out, Cringle slammed the brakes of the Fleetwood hard, tires shrieking on the road surface. He pulled into the space with inches to spare, reversed back and cut the motor. Eyes popping, the man in the Chevy wound down his window. His face looked like a red beet as he shouted across to Cringle.

"That was my space!"

"Beat it, Buster!" said Cringle, slowly turning his face toward the man at the wheel of the other car. The driver opened his mouth once or twice as though to say something and caught sight of the scar. He shut his mouth suddenly, turned white, nodded and drove off rapidly. He didn't look back. Cringle chuckled to himself. He pulled his hat forward over his eyes and settled down to read the sports section.

Half an hour passed. The man in the striped suit finished reading the baseball scores and turned to the *Gazette*. He idly flipped the pages. His eyes expressed appreciation as he looked at the three column spread of Diana Palmer in a pin-up pose in her bikini by the pool of her Westchester home. He glanced at the caption underneath. It said: HUNTING THE SCORPIA-DIANA PALMER: see column one.

Cringle sat up, pushing his hat to the back of his head. He read on, his original purpose in parking by the sidewalk obviously forgotten. The first paragraph of Dinah Mulvaney's story made him jerk forward; the matchstick he had been chewing fell from between his teeth to the floor of the car unnoticed.

The story began, "Lovely Diana Palmer, the Westchester Olympic athlete and explorer, has a new hobby. She is attending night classes at the University and is studying medieval history. But medieval history with a difference. She is trying to trace the origins of an eighteenth century pirate band, the Scorpia."

Cringle finished the story and read it again. He folded the newspaper and put it carefully on the seat beside him. The hard, unrelenting look had returned to his face. He sat thinking for a moment. Then he looked at the newspaper again. The Palmer story had a footnote. He got out of the car and walked back to the news-stand.

"You got a yesterday's *Gazette* left, Mose?" he asked the proprietor.

"Sure, Mr. Cringle," said the little man. "At least, I'm pretty sure we have one. Hold it."

He scratched the pile of papers waiting to be returned. A few moments later he came up with the paper. He waved away the proffered coin.

"A pleasure, Mr. Cringle. Besides, you just tipped me."

"Sure, I did, creep," Cringle said. He smiled a cold smile. "I was just testing you."

He got back in the Fleetwood and drove out of town.

Cringle hunched over the wheel, fighting the steering on the corners as he took the big car up to high speed. Presently, he turned off the turnpike onto a rough, gravel road that led into the hills. He dropped the speed down to a crawl as the tires drummed over rocky ridges and sank into potholes. It took him more than half an hour, climbing all the time, before he came in sight of his destination.

The tires thudded over the slats of a rough-hewn timber bridge that spanned a torrent foaming white over dark boulders. Then, Cringle turned uphill for the last time and pulled the Fleetwood off the road into a private drive. He stopped the Cadillac in the big half-moon forecourt of a rambling old two-story farmhouse whose frame was sagging with age and neglect. The great boarded porch seemed stooped with the weight of the years as he went up the steps to the paint-blistered front door with its curved skylight.

He put the key into a well-oiled lock and went through into a cavernous hall that was lit by a single bulb from a ceiling fixture. The light shone on nineteenth century furniture covered with dust. Choking clouds of it rose from the worn carpet as Cringle padded up the staircase. It creaked ominously with every step he took. He ascended two flights and stopped in front of a door from which emanated a pale yellow light. He knocked three times. A key turned in the lock and the door opened.

The room into which Cringle blinked his way was in marked contrast to the staircase he had just left. It had cream-painted walls; modern, comfortable furniture, and his feet sank into luxurious carpeting. It was like stepping a hundred years ahead in time without warning. The man who had opened the door took his place again on a comfortable couch and fingered the leather cover of a book he had just put down.

He was about fifty and had a smooth, bald, egg-shaped head. Below his vast expanse of brow a broad, soft face complemented the upper half of his features. His mouth was wide and fleshy; he had strong yellow teeth and the tufts of hair at his ears gave him the look of a benevolent uncle. The resemblance ended when he raised his eyes to look at Cringle, who sank into a chair in front of him. The eyes were hard and deadly, those of a born killer, and their ruthless grey pupils drilled into Cringle's own. Hardened as he was, Cringle felt a curious little shiver whenever he looked into them.

The plump man had a comfortable body to match his face; he wore a lightweight grey suit which sat baggily on his big frame, a flaming red tie over a black and white stripped shirt, and red carpet slippers. A big cigar protruded from one corner of his wide mouth, and every once in a while a hot ash would drop from it onto the front of the big man's coat Then he would absently brush the ashes away; but the jacket retained a greyish hue.

"Is everything O.K.?" the fat man asked quietly, leaning back on the couch.

"That depends on what you mean," said Cringle in a hard, cold voice.

"Give me a straight answer," said the fat man.

"Have you seen these newspaper items, Otto?" said the blond

man, waving the two copies of the *Gazette*.

"No, and it's hardly likely that I'll be able to read them if you continue to wave them about," said the fat man jovially.

"Let's hope you'll be as relaxed when you've read them," granted Cringle. "They're about the Scorpia."

The fat man's eyes hooded suddenly, as he dropped his lids over them. Then, the grey pupils were drilling into Cringle's eyes. The atmosphere in the room suddenly seemed to become electrified.

"You don't really mean it, Cringle," he said softly. "You'd better read them to me."

Cringle gulped; his throat seemed constricted and he swallowed once or twice. He was reminded vividly of the little man in the Chevy earlier that evening. Otto had the same effect on him. He unfolded the papers, finding the palms of his hands sticky with sweat.

"There were two articles," he explained. "One yesterday, one tonight. Both about Diana Palmer, the Olympic swimmer. She lives in Westchester. Apparently, she's been studying the history of the Scorpia at college."

Otto had closed his eyes and sat with his hands folded across his fat paunch.

"Go on, Cringle," he said with a sigh. "I'm still waiting." Cringle read the two articles aloud. There was a long silence when he finished.

"That's not all," Cringle went on, when the fat man showed no signs of continuing the conversation.

"I looked at today's television guide earlier. The Palmer girl is going to be on a local talk show tonight. Do you suppose they'll ask her about her Scorpia research?"

"I really have no idea," said Otto calmly. He opened his eyes suddenly and the steely gaze was like a searchlight in the room. "What time?"

Cringle fumbled with the paper.

"Channel Five," he said. "Nine-fifteen."

He consulted his watch.

"That's ten minutes from now."

"You'd better tune in then," said Otto.

He leaned back on the couch as Cringle fumbled with the knobs of the TV set.

"I know two things, Cringle," the fat man went on, as though talking to himself. "One is that Diana Palmer had better not do any talking about Scorpia on television or she'll be in trouble."

"What's the other?" said Cringle, the image on the screen growing clearer with his manipulations.

"It's your job to keep her from talking, Cringle," said Otto.

His deadly gaze seemed to wither his subordinate as it passed over him.

"You know as well as I that no one talks about Scorpia without risk of sudden death."

He leaned forward, his stare pinning Cringle almost physically to the front of the set.

"If you don't stop her, Cringle, you will also be in very serious trouble."

CHAPTER 5

Castle Toeplitz

O tto gave an impatient sigh as Cringle continued to fiddle with the dials of the TV set.

"We'll miss the program, you clown," he said softly. "Then I shall be annoyed."

"Sorry, Otto," said Cringle, nervously. He relaxed as a clear picture came into focus. He adjusted the sound and went to sit at the other end of the couch as introductory music announced the local news program. Otto sat motionless as two boring items on animal husbandry and teenage education were dealt with.

Then both men stiffened as the announcer said, "Now, education with a difference. The Olympic swimming champion and woman explorer, Miss Diana Palmer of our own Westchester Palmers, has come up with some unusual facts after researching for the University's medieval history course."

Then followed a two minute analysis of Diana Palmer's public career; some film of her home and an interview with her mother and Uncle David, who said crisply, "Everything my niece does is news."

The screen dissolved to a panel with the interviewer in the middle, Diana Palmer on his left and Miss Welch on his right. Miss Welch was saying, "I was surprised. It's the first time any of my students has had her research mentioned in a newspaper social column."

The interviewer and the studio audience laughed. Diana Palmer was speaking now.

"At first I thought I was studying an ancient pirate band destroyed over four hundred years ago," she said.

Cringle felt sweat running down the palm of his right hand. He wiped it surreptitiously on his trousers.

"What do you mean by that, Miss Palmer?" the interviewer went on.

A close-up of Diana Palmer followed as she replied, "This was a band of ferocious criminals. They began as pirates, originally, and I've traced them almost up to modern times. I believe they might still exist."

"It sounds incredible, Miss Palmer," the announcer said. "You are certainly following an original line of research."

"Yes," Miss Welch broke in. "And it's also the first time that such an apparently academic subject has attracted such publicity."

"What do you consider the significance of your discoveries, if any?" the commentator queried.

"Who knows?" said Diana brightly. "I haven't reached any conclusions as yet."

"But do you believe that a related and unchanged band of criminals could continue to exist through hundreds of years?" said the commentator.

Diana shrugged.

"Anything is possible. But it's difficult to tell at this stage. I have a lot more checking to do before I can come to any definite conclusion."

"What do you think, Miss Welch?" the commentator continued.

"I agree with Diana," Miss Welch replied. "Anything is possible. I think she has chosen a most extraordinary subject to research. I admit I didn't think much of her choice at first. But like most things Diana Palmer sets her mind to, some amazing facts have emerged. I only wish I had a few more students like her."

Otto sat impassive as the interview went on. Cringle glanced at him from time to time, but it was impossible to read anything from his flabby features. Only his grey eyes were alive. He sat relaxed on the couch, his plump hands folded in his lap, the smoke from his cigar going straight up to the ceiling in the still air of the room.

"Miss Palmer," the commentator continued with a smile, "what would happen if you did discover that Scorpia was still in operation in some parts of the world?"

"Well, I hardly think it's possible that I could uncover anything that the International police wouldn't be aware of," said Diana diffidently.

"But if I uncover anything concrete, then, of course, I would give my information to them."

"And you intend to go on with your research?" the interviewer asked.

"Of course," said Diana. "I have a great deal more material to sift through. And, naturally, Miss Welch will expect a first-rate paper after all this publicity."

There was another burst of laughter from the studio audience and as background music began, the announcer said smilingly, "Well, we'll try and bring you the sequel to this story in a week or two. In the meantime here's a late news report. . ."

His voice faded and the screen went blank as Cringle turned the set off. He went back to the couch, looking anxiously at the slumped form of Otto.

"You see why I was worried. . ." he began.

"Shut up," said Otto softly but authoritatively. There was so much menace in his voice that Cringle fell silent.

"I must think about this," Otto went on.

He turned his deadly grey eyes toward his subordinate.

"And we can't have any bungling at this stage."

Cringle cleared his throat awkwardly. He thought it wiser not to interrupt.

The fat man got up abruptly. Despite his bulk he moved as swiftly and almost as gracefully as a ballet dancer. He glanced over at Cringle, saw with approval that the blond man was watching him intently. He relaxed his forbidding attitude.

"You were right to bring this to my attention. Cringle," he said. "It could be serious."

He went on pacing up and down for another few moments.

"On the other hand," the fat man went on, "we don't want to make fools of ourselves. As sure as my name is Otto Koch I can't afford to make any mistakes with Center. They've been getting very touchy lately."

"That's why I thought it might be important, Otto," said Cringle ingratiatingly. "You think we ought to contact them?"

"My mind is moving along those lines," Koch said, shooting his subordinate another quelling glance. "But let's analyze the situation first"

"Here's a little girl doing a history paper," said Koch in a faraway voice as though he was talking in his sleep. "Nothing special in that, except that she happens to be a famous personality, which makes her news. So the local sheet runs a few paragraphs about her hobby of studying history."

He opened his eyes suddenly, fixing Cringle with a glance that made him flinch. He turned back to his glass.

"Unfortunately she's come across the Scorpia in her research. And pirate bands who continue to thrive through hundreds of years are rather unusual. Do you follow me, Cringle?"

"Certainly, Otto," said Cringle, looking up quickly.

"Pay attention then," said Koch. His voice cracked like a pistol in the quiet room.

"So that attracts the attention of a television station, that runs a talk show beamed into possibly 20,000 homes."

Koch picked up his glass again and looked into its depths reflectively.

"That's twenty-thousand possibilities too many," he said. "So where do we go from here? Or rather, where does Diana Palmer go from here?"

He got up again and stood in the center of the room.

"Now are the TV people going to run another show in two weeks? And if they are, will Miss Palmer have come up with anything? In other words, will she have uncovered anything else about Scorpia by then?"

"What is there to find out about Scorpia in books?" Cringle asked.

"I don't know," said Otto imperturbably. "But are we justified in taking that risk?"

He started pacing up and down the quiet room, interrupting his sentry walk by an occasional sip from the glass picked up from the arm of the couch.

"Supposing network television gets onto this?" he said, turning back to Cringle.

"Diana Palmer's famous. It's a possibility. And Scorpia's existence might then become public knowledge throughout the country."

He shook his head and finished off the drink.

"No, no. On reconsideration, we cannot risk it. I read the situation as a Red Alert."

Cringle straightened up and put his glass down as Otto Koch drew himself up to his full height.

"We'll contact Center and ask for instructions," he said crisply.

Colonel Crang's massive head, like a pineapple on top of his bulky body, appeared above the Castle battlements so suddenly that the sentry below, taken unaware, almost dropped his rifle as he came to attention. But Crang had no time for him today. He gazed down from the Castle walls, raising his eyes from the paved courtyard, to where the dark blue of the sea met the lighter rim of the sky beyond.

The Colonel's tanned features were set and stern as he gazed around him. He was in charge of security and the Baron had been increasingly critical of late. He sighed and resumed his solitary pacing along the battlements. His white tropical cap was surmounted with an eagle and crest denoting his rank. His thick, black mustache dropped across his cheeks, making the whiteness of his teeth almost startling, when he opened his mouth to converse or give an order.

He wore a light grey tropical uniform which carried his badges of rank, and the gold epaulettes denoted that he was also the Baron's personal equerry. His figure was so broad that he looked almost squat, although he was just a shade under six feet tall. A Browning revolver in a brown leather holster was buckled round his waist, and his boots were polished so brightly that they reflected the sun like a mirror. Scarlet piping ran down the sides of his trousers indicating his rank to subordinates long before he approached them.

Down below, the sea broke softly on wicked-looking rocks which rose to a craggy precipice over two hundred feet high, on top of which Castle Toeplitz was perched. The castle itself, centuries old, with its turreted towers and serrated battlements, was smothered by vegetation and tropical vines, but even the scarlet flowers of the vines could do little to soften its harsh and forbidding lines. Once a ruin, the Castle had now been lavishly restored and garrisoned.

Crang paused at the end of his tour of the ramparts and frowned. From this angle he could look across the miles of thick green jungle of the island itself. He took the stub of his cigar out of his mouth with an impatient gesture and flicked it over the ramparts. It made a little arc of sparks in the air and then scattered as it hit a projecting stone buttress and disappeared into the jungle below.

Crang consulted his wrist watch. He frowned again. He was two minutes late on his rounds because of his daydreaming. He started walking smartly around the angle of the parapet and down a flight of thick, twisting steps that led to a lower level. Here, the incongruous mass of a steel radio mast jutted out of the stonework high above him. He hurried over to a red-painted door set in the ancient wall.

The door bore the legend in white letters: RADIO SHACK. Crang opened the door and climbed a narrow, winding staircase that was lit only by small, glassed-in slits that had once been used for firing arrows. The air was dry and musty, as though no one had breathed it for centuries.

Presently, Crang came to a stone landing above which a solitary electric bulb burned in a metal socket set into the solid wall. There was a grey-painted door here. Crang turned the handle and walked in. The high, thin notes of morse code split the air and there was a humming and a crackling noise. An officer turned from a table and saluted as Crang approached.

"Message just coming through from Otto Koch," he whispered.

Colonel Crang nodded and sat down in a padded leather chair. He stared over to where a soldier hunched beneath the steel circlet of his earphones writing the message on the signal pad in front of him. In rows around the rough stone walls were grey-painted transmitters and receivers.

The only compartment in use was one which had UNITED STATES painted on a board screwed to the wall above it. The message continued for about ten minutes. The officer clicked his teeth in impatience as the operator bent over his morse key again. He asked for a repeat on a section of the message. The officer was already leaning over the operator's shoulder, copying the first two groups of coded letters on his own pad. He went to the signal book and flipped the pages.

Then he turned to the Colonel, his eyes wide and surprised.

"It's a Red Alert, sir," he said. "I'm afraid you'll have to decode the message yourself. I don't have the authority."

"I thank you. Lieutenant," said Crang smoothly, his mind exploring the possibilities. He was too old a hand to get excited about Red Alerts. His past experience had proved that they were seldom justified, especially with the operators they were forced to use these days; they seemed to think any sign of police activity called for the highest priority to Center. On the other hand, Otto Koch was one of the most skilled and experienced operators in the Western Hemisphere. He seldom got excited about anything unless it was out of the ordinary.

Crang frowned. He had better decode it at once. But his tones had their accustomed smoothness and control as he told the Lieutenent, "I will take the codebooks into your office. Perhaps you would be good enough to bring the balance of the message in when it is completed."

The officer saluted again and bent over the operator's shoulder as Crang gathered up the books. He made himself comfortable at the desk in the Lieutenant's small office and looked idly out of the window as he waited. The view from here was most disappointing. But then it would be, as Crang's own suite had one of the finest and most spectacular views in the Castle, except when compared to the Baron's.

He waited five minutes, and only the soft drumming of his stubby fingers on the desk indicated his inward impatience. He brushed aside the Lieutenant's apologies and took the coded message from him with a muttered thanks. He was pleased to see that the officer had torn off the four sheets beneath the top copy, thus preventing the operator from reading the impressions of the letters and figures beneath. Crang now detached these sheets and set fire to them with a lighter taken from the pocket of his uniform jacket. He watched them crumple to powder in the metal wastebasket at his feet.

Then he set to work decoding Koch's message. It took him less than fifteen minutes. He had not absorbed the meaning of it and it took another minute or two before the essence of the decoded version became clear. He put the original signal in his pocket and prepared a typed decoded version for the Baron.

He then burned the balance of the papers so that only the operator's coded signal and his own typed version in English remained. There was a knock on the door as he finished. The Lieutenant entered, saluting.

His face tried to conceal his curiosity.

"I trust it's nothing serious, sir?"

"It will be serious if you don't stop prying into top-secret signals," said the Colonel. "I've warned you before. The Cipher Officer at Toeplitz cannot be too discreet."

The Lieutenant turned a dull pink.

"Sorry, sir," he said. "It won't happen again."

Crang smiled briefly.

"Just make sure it doesn't," he said.

He saluted and went out. He felt a sense of apprehension as he climbed the battlements on his way to the Baron's private apartments.

CHAPTER 6

Baron Sojin's Eyrie

There were two sentries on duty at the base of the strange, turreted tower which soared more than fifty feet from the center of the highest courtyard of the castle. They both presented arms as Crang hurried across toward them. The Baron Sojin's apartments were in the top of the tower commanding the highest point of the island. Just below the Baron's quarters was the armory and below that, the members of the Baron's selected Household Guard had their own apartments on the courtyard level. Crang smiled again. The Baron's own chambers were almost invulnerable.

Crang's suite was just below this final courtyard, overlooking the sea. He was only a minute or so from the Baron if he should need him, and it often pleased the strange master of the Island of Scorpia to call the Colonel out in the middle of the night. He was used to that, however. It was what he was paid for. And his salary was on an astronomical level as befitted an officer who was in the Baron's confidence and his right-hand man. Now he saluted again as the guards presented arms.

"Colonel Crang to see the Baron on urgent personal business," he said into the voice-box set into the wall at the side of the sentry shelter. The sentries knew well enough who he was, and the Baron probably already knew he was on his way up, but protocol had to be observed. A metallic voice echoed back from the metal grill in the side of the box. "Will the Colonel please go on up."

The Colonel recognized the duty Commander of the Guard who had probably scrutinized him through the closed-circuit television camera. The sentries saluted Crang again as the Colonel slid back the steel door in the wall. He got into the mahogany panelled elevator cage and pressed the button which bore the symbol of the Baron's own quarters. He had to use an electronic key in the elevator circuit before he could operate the button. The elevator shot swiftly upward. Through a small window at the side of the cage Crang could now see the castle and the surface of a gently undulating sea.

As he went higher he could then see the Baron's personal standard, a scarlet Scorpion on a yellow background, flying from the Castle flagpole, a sure sign that the Baron was in residence. The cage jerked to a halt. Crang waited until the electronic time locks operated, then pressed the button which activated the doors. He went through into a metal corridor. His feet echoed eerily as he marched along it There was a thick glass wall at one end, and through it a magnificent panorama of the whole south side of the island was visible.

Crang never failed to get a thrill at the sight, but he had no time to admire the view today. A small television screen next to the chrome steel door blinked into life, and the figure of the Baron surveyed him. The voice echoed tinnily through the speaker.

"I trust you have a good reason for disturbing me at this time of day, Colonel?"

"Indeed, sir," said Crang, directing his voice toward the metal microphone at the side of the door. He knew his own image would be visible on the monitor screen on the Baron's desk.

"We have just received a Red Alert from the United States."

"Indeed!"

The Baron's voice was cool and well-modulated. His figure on the TV screen stirred slightly at the desk.

"Yes, that would appear to be sufficient reason for your appearance in my Headquarters at this hour. You may enter."

The screen went blank as the chrome steel door started to rumble back. The Colonel marched through. He found himself in a tropical jungle. Plants writhed upward toward the light, and scarlet and yellow flowers gave off a sickly odor. The large conservatory windows repeated the spectacular view seen from the corridor outside. Crang's feet clattered across a metal ramp as he picked his way through the riot of vegetation. He opened the glass door at the far side and went through into a very different world.

The room in which he now stood was more than forty feet long. The ancient stone walls from which it had been originally formed were now encased in intricately carved panelling. Curved windows of toughened glass gave the occupants views in three directions. The magnificent oak beams of the ceiling had been retained. The room was like the bow of a ship. Where Crang stood was the broader part leading to midships, while the walls gradually became sharper in angle, leading the eye to where the Baron's desk stood on a dais made of polished wood.

Steps led up to it. Beyond, a large, spiral staircase made of teak curved upwards into the dusk leading to Baron Sojin's personal quarters. Books in a dozen different languages glimmered in fitted bookcases around the room. On the dais, near the Baron's desk, were all the electronic and communications aids he used to help him run his vast criminal empire. Below the staircase, taking up more than ten feet of the room's length, was a massive illuminated map of the world, on which the Baron could see at a glance the extent and scope of Scorpia's rule.

He stood up as Crang approached the steps of the dais and indicated a leather chair to one side.

"Do sit down, my dear Colonel," he said in his distinctive voice. A slight Central European accent betrayed his origins.

"I trust that your news will not spoil my day."

"I hope so too, sir," said the Colonel, settling himself back in the armchair and reaching into his pocket.

"But I felt it my duty to come straight here to report."

"Quite right, Colonel," said Baron Sojin softly.

He was a man of more than normal height, thin but with broad shoulders and a deep chest that denoted a man in fine physical condition, an athlete almost. His forehead was high and broad and his chestnut colored hair was receding. The effect was minimized, however, by the use of a razor, which cropped it fashionably short. The Baron's eyes were a startling blue with long curling lashes. He looked to be about forty years of age, though it was difficult to tell.

He had an even, deeply-tanned skin stretched smoothly over high cheekbones. His nose was strong and broad, his teeth white and clean. It was only his mouth that gave him away. Wide and slit-like, it revealed his ruthless, tempestuous nature. The lips were bloodless and bleached, and when he smiled, which was frequently, it was like a mirthless slot opening in his face. The Baron's origin was obscure.

Colonel Crang, studying him for the hundredth time, was not inclined to question it. It was not healthy. He had no experience of the Baron's temper himself, but he had heard from others. One of his predecessors in office, he understood, had disappeared. A year later, his remains had been found impaled on the branch of a tree in the jungle far below the castle. Men of the garrison whispered that the man had been pushed from the Baron's own quarters. The Colonel did not doubt that it might well be so. But the man was probably a fool. He himself hated inefficiency and he would not tolerate it in his subordinates.

Now he stirred on his chair and came up with the typed sheet giving Otto Koch's message.

"This is from Otto Koch in District No. 84, sir," he said crisply.

"There is, apparently, a young woman named Diana Palmer, who is something of a celebrity. She lives in Westchester and is an Olympic swimmer, scholar and explorer."

He paused, aware that the Baron was smiling.

"You interest me, Colonel," he said. "This girl is young and beautiful, yes?"

The Colonel coughed and shifted in his chair.

"So I understand, sir," he said.

The Baron sat back in his chair and rubbed his hands together.

"Admirable," he said. "And this girl is likely to give us some trouble or we would not have a message about her? Correct?"

"Exactly so, sir," said the Colonel, blinking.

The Baron's intuitions were quite uncanny at times. He was a formidable opponent. The Colonel was glad that they were both working for the same side.

"The girl has, apparently, been studying seventeenth and eighteenth century history," he went on, aware that the Baron was listening intently to his every word.

"She specialized in pirate bands and other Brotherhoods of lawlessness. During her research she stumbled on some references to the Scorpia in ancient documents."

The Colonel blinked again at the Baron's reaction. His leather and steel chair creaked ominously as Sojin sat bolt upright and fixed his blue eyes on a point somewhere beyond the Colonel's right shoulder.

"Do go on, Crang," the Baron said softly.

"This is the point, sir," Crang continued. "This girl is a celebrity in America. Everything she does is news. Koch first picked up some items about her hobby in the local newspaper. Now the television people have got hold of it, and she's been speaking about Scorpia on her local station to a fairly wide audience. According to her, the Scorpia was not destroyed four hundred years ago as was believed. She hopes to prove that it survives to this day."

"As indeed it does, my dear Colonel," said the Baron in a deceptively mild voice.

The Colonel was astonished at the Baron's reaction. He had expected some violent outburst from this mercurial man. The Baron was ominously quiet, however, for such a powerful personality. He sat back in his chair again and smiled slowly at the Colonel.

"You are certain, Colonel, are you not, that the Palmer girl spoke on a local television station and not on a nationwide network?"

"Koch was quite specific on that point, Baron," said Crang stiffly. He prided himself on his exactitude, and even the Baron could not criticize him on that score.

"You do see the importance. Colonel?" the Baron continued.

He got up; his tall, thin figure looking even taller. He wore a red, silk robe over blue, uniform trousers and a white, silk shirt, and the robe emphasized his height. He went to look silently out of one of the curved windows at the magnificent vista of sea and jungle below him.

"This is a sight I never tire of, Crang," he said over his shoulder. "When the affairs of Scorpia are more than usually pressing, then I come to stand here, and the world and its problems fall into proper perspective."

Crang did not reply and after a moment the Baron said, with a nervous jerk of his head, "Do come and look, Colonel."

It was an order, not a request and Crang crossed swiftly to his side. It was indeed a breath-taking sight and, though Crang had seen it many times, each time seemed more spectacular than before. Both men were silent for a long minute. Then the Baron turned away.

He put his hand on the Colonel's arm.

"This matter of the girl and the Scorpia."

He went to sit back at his desk.

"It is true we exist. And it is equally true that we do not wish the world to know this. But was Koch's information really worth a Red Alert? He is a good man and we value his talents, nevertheless. A commendation then, in your reply, and a gentle hint that the situation would more correctly have been indicated by an Amber."

Crang nodded. "Noted, sir," he said.

"Excellent, Colonel Crang," the Baron went on. "Our reactions must not be too violent in this instance. The situation could be dangerous. Instruct Koch to stop the girl—in as gentle a manner as possible."

"Very good, sir."

Crang inclined his head and clicked his heels. He paused, wondering whether the Baron had any further instructions.

Sojin smiled gently. Anyone but Crang would have shuddered, the expression seemed like a smile on a dead face.

"You may leave now, Colonel," he said.

He waited until the Colonel's echoing footsteps down the hall had died away. The door closed behind his subordinate, and the ruler of Scorpia crossed to his desk. He flipped on the switch of the closed circuit TV. Crang's impassive face stared back at him as he went down in the elevator.

Sojin flipped the switch off again and went back to study the magnificent view. For the first time in his life he felt lonely amid the splendors of Castle Toeplitz and his private kingdom of Scorpia.

The girl Diana Palmer sounded interesting. A woman of spirit evidently, as her accomplishments indicated. Yes, they would have to go gently at first. He smiled again. But interesting, very interesting.

CHAPTER 7

Orders from Toeplitz

Cringle's scar twitched and pulled his eyelid more to the side than usual. He sat hunched over the morse key in the boarded loft room of the old house, his hard face twisted into a knot of concentration. From the earphones, clamped to his blond hair, came the rapid high-pitched tone of the signals coming over the thousands of miles that separated receiver and transmitter. He perspired slightly as his hand faltered on the signal pad, slurring the outline of the figures.

He rapidly broke into the transmission with a series of long notes and then signalled for a repetition of the group. Otto Koch sat on a hard, wooden chair in a corner of the attic and watched him benevolently. His fat, bland face looked more like an egg than ever. The acrid, blue smoke from his cigar rose slowly toward the ceiling and he seemed oblivious to the ash which dropped on his red tie.

It was impossible to tell from his expression what he was thinking as he listened to the staccato of the morse symbols which meant nothing to him. His pudgy hand seemed to caress the thick pile of decoding books on the bench at his side. His grey eyes were entirely without emotion as he gazed patiently upward, watching the ascent of his own smoke whorls.

The transmission finally came to an end. Cringle signalled

an acknowledgment and then switched off the equipment. He gave a heavy sigh of relief and pulled the pad towards him. He started carefully recopying the letters into a more legible form for Koch to read.

"I've become a little rusty since my days in the Signal Corps, Otto," he said nervously.

Koch said nothing but continued to wait in the same patient manner until the scratching of his subordinate's pencil finally ceased. He took the sheets from Cringle's hand and gazed at the blond man pointedly. Cringle flushed, as his gaze went downward to the bench before him. He suddenly understood the other's meaning.

He tore off the top sheets of the signal pad and bundled them together with his first rough copy of the message. He set fire to the sheets with a lighter and ground the flaming mass to ashes on the floor. He made sure not a fragment of paper remained. Then he got a dustpan and brush and swept it up.

While he was doing this, Koch was busy with the message and the decoding books on the bench. He sat, oblivious of Cringle's movements, until halfway through when the latter heard him give a sudden click of annoyance with his tongue.

"Well, well, Cringle," Otto said, breaking his long silence. "So Center feels my signal should have been an Amber Alert. So be it. Perhaps it looks like that from Scorpia but it's slightly more dangerous at this end."

He turned the searchlight of his piercing, grey eyes on Cringle.

"Let us hope that the Baron has his priorities right,"

His pudgy fingers beat a tattoo on the bench.

"Of course, he is not often wrong. But even so, the man on the spot is usually in a far better position to evaluate the situation."

Tiny spots of red stood out on his cheeks, and Cringle guessed that his chief had been slightly wounded by the tone of the message. But caution prompted him to remain silent. So he said nothing, and after a moment or two Otto went back to his decoding. Cringle resumed his place at the bench and lit a cigarette. Presently, Otto stirred and scanned the entire message again.

"More and more curious," he told the walls.

"Meaning what?" Cringle asked.

"Meaning, Cringle, that we're to soft-pedal the entire matter." Cringle screwed up his ugly face in surprise.

"What do you mean, soft-pedal?" he said aggressively. "This dame is liable to blow Scorpia clear into the open with her running-off at the mouth."

"Are you giving the orders here, or is the Baron?" said Otto softly.

The blond man fell silent.

"I was only expressing my opinion," he said after a moment or two.

"An opinion unasked for and usually faulty," said Otto ponderously. "No, this calls for more thought."

"Am I allowed to know the message?" Cringle asked.

"I don't see why not," said Otto benevolently. "But it's difficult to see what other interpretation could be made."

He picked up the sheet and studied it again.

"The essence is in the final paragraph," he added.

"Stop her gently. Arouse no suspicion."

Cringle grimaced in disbelief.

"How can we stop her gently?" he asked in his turn.

"And without suspicion. It doesn't make sense."

"Nevertheless, Cringle, those are the instructions," said Otto Koch softly. "And who are we to question the orders of Center?"

"I didn't mean that, chief," said Cringle hastily.

Otto smiled briefly. It seemed to make his face look like that of a benevolent priest.

"I'm sure you didn't, Cringle," he said. "But you have a point. It is a rather delicate situation. And it must be handled properly. Otherwise, there might be dire consequences."

He hooded his eyes again in the way that filled Cringle with alarm.

"For you in the first instance," he warned. "And myself in the second," he added softly, turning back to study the signal sheet.

"So we must make doubly sure there are no slip-ups. What are your ideas on how to handle the situation delicately."

Cringle shifted uneasily in his chair.

"I haven't had much time to think about it," he said.

"Think about it now," said Koch patiently. "You have about thirty seconds."

"But that's unfair, Chief!" Cringle burst out involuntarily.

Otto smiled again. Cringle shuddered at his expression,

"It's an unfair world, Cringle," Otto said.

He settled himself back, his hands comfortably clasped over his stomach.

"I'm sure you'll think of something."

Diana Palmer ran lightly down the stairs as Uncle David came through the drawing room door. He had his pipe in the corner of his mouth and he was carrying a copy of the Westchester Gazette in his right hand. Diana knew that he was on his way to her mother's sewing room to join her for an hour, a custom they invariably followed at this time of the day.

David Palmer pretended astonishment as he looked up at the hurried figure of his niece. She glanced at her wrist watch as she reached the bottom of the stairs and saw that it was already a quarter to seven. Her uncle read her thoughts.

Would you like me to drive you over, Diana?"

"No thanks, Uncle Dave," the girl replied. "I'll walk. I'll make it easily if I don't waste time."

"Ah, well," said David Palmer with a smile. "It's all very fine for Olympic athletes! You'll prefer the car at my age."

"We'll see, Grandpappy!" said Diana mischievously, as she swung out of the house. She crossed the boulevard and walked on the other side this evening. It was more shadowy there and the dimmer lighting was soothing after the brilliant glare of the house. There were few people about at this hour. People were either preparing for dinner or on their way home from business, and it was too early for theater or movie traffic. It was just a few minutes after the hour when Diana arrived at the college.

Miss Welch greeted her like an old friend, and they spent a few minutes before the session discussing the TV show.

"I've had letters from several people and sixteen phone calls," said Miss Welch excitedly, with just the faintest suspicion of a flush on her face. "I feel like a celebrity!"

"I'm glad you enjoyed it, Miss Welch," said Diana. "I thought the broadcast was well-handled, and it certainly was an interesting experience."

"Will we be asked to do another, if you come up with any more information during your research?" questioned Miss Welch, patting a stray hair on her forehead into place. She looked ten years younger, Diana thought. "I don't see why not, if I've got fresh material," said Diana. "I'm looking forward to it. The producer said he would call me next week."

"Great!" said Miss Welch, suddenly aware that the other members of the class were watching Diana and herself closely.

"I beg your pardon, ladies and gentlemen," she called. "I didn't realize the time. We'll begin immediately."

Diana went to her desk and got out her notebooks and reference works. The session passed slowly tonight; the references were sparse. She seemed to have reached a stodgy period in the late nineteenth century, and when the bell rang at the end she realized that she had not gleaned a single new fact about that elusive and tantalizing band, the Scorpia.

She glanced up, acknowledging the good-nights of her colleagues, and then became aware that Miss Welch was back at her elbow.

"How did it go tonight, Diana?" she asked.

Diana shrugged. "Slowly and rather dully," she said. "I think it's about time I got started on the term paper. It looks as though I'm scraping the bottom of the barrel." "Well," said Miss Welch, smiling, "you've had more publicity than a Nobel prize-winner."

"I didn't mean that," Diana explained. "I've become really interested in the Scorpia now, and just when I seemed on the verge of a breakthrough, the information dried up."

"It happens to all historians, amateur and professional," said Miss Welch, following Diana to the door. "The main thing is not to get discouraged. It's usually when one's on the point of giving up that something unusual happens."

"That's true," agreed Diana, switching off the library light as the two women closed the door behind them.

"The only trouble here is that I don't know how much more material there is," Diana went on as they walked to the main entrance hall of the University. "It's getting pretty sparse and I have a horrible suspicion I'm coming to the end of all the known records."

"Don't give up, Diana," said Miss Welch brightly as they picked their way down the main steps.

"Remember, all the material we sent for from the County Archives should be here soon."

"I'd forgotten that," said Diana, as the two women paused on the boulevard before parting to go their separate ways.

"Anyway, don't take it too seriously," Miss Welch added. "It's all good fun, and the University has never had so much publicity before! And our enrollment for next term has increased measurably."

"As long as it's done some good," said Diana laughing.

The two women said good-night, and Diana watched as she saw Miss Welch's sprightly form dart across the road and onto the opposite sidewalk. Her hand fluttered goodbye, and then she disappeared into a side street as Diana turned toward home. She was busily mulling over the thoughts in her mind, so that she hardly noticed where she walked. It was true that the Scorpia—and the shadowy figure of Kit Walker—had been occupying a great deal of her mind lately.

Her face softened as she thought of Kit again, and she instinctively slowed her pace.

She was on a dark section of the sidewalk, where heavily-blossomed trees sagged down toward the cement path. A sudden squealing of brakes cut through her reverie. She glanced up to see the gleaming bulk of a Cadillac blocking out the light from the opposite sidewalk.

A hard-faced man with blond hair and a scar on the side of his face rolled down the window. His eyes glittered dully in the gloom.

"Miss Palmer," he said in a harsh, dead voice. "I'd like a word with you."

CHAPTER 8

Early Warning

Cringle's face momentarily softened as he absorbed the details of Diana Palmer's appearance. He slid farther over on the seat so that he could clearly see this celebrated woman athlete.

Diana drew closer to the Cadillac.

"I'm Diana Palmer," she said. "What is it?"

Cringle lit a cigarette. The flaring match momentarily made a cavernous mask of his face. His scar stood out lividly. Diana suddenly shivered.

"You've been writing a paper..." Cringle began, killing the motor of the car.

"Yes, that's right," said Diana. She laughed. "I suppose you caught the TV show."

"Right," said Cringle, nodding. "But you didn't let me finish, lady." He cleared his throat. "You've chosen a certain subject," he went on.

Diana's face clouded.

"Oh, you're from a newspaper," she said. "I don't usually give interviews on the sidewalk. And it is rather late."

"I'm not a reporter," said Cringle. "Just listen carefully. You're researching Scorpia."

His eyes, hard and glittering, bored into Diana's.

"Forget Scorpia! Get it?"

Diana felt confused.

"I'm afraid I don't," she said. "What do you mean?" "What I

said, lady," Cringle continued in his dead voice.

"But why should research on an ancient pirate band like the Scorpia interest you?" said Diana, looking round the deserted street.

Cringle's face went white.

"From now on, don't even mention that name, lady," he said.

He slid his forefinger across his throat. The gesture was so sinister that Diana instinctively started back from the car door.

"Forget it," Cringle hissed blackly.

He turned on the Cadillac's motor and idled it.

"This is the first and last warning, Diana Palmer."

He gunned the car off down the street. It turned the corner with tires shrieking, and disappeared. The whole thing had happened so quickly that Diana had no time even to read the license plate. Then she realized that the blond man had switched the lights of the automobile off so that she wouldn't have been able to read the license number anyway. It was only when he was turning the corner, too far away for her to read them, that he switched on the lights.

Diana stood irresolute for a moment. There was a determined look on her face. Had Cringle seen it, he would not have felt so confident as he turned the big car back in the direction of Otto Koch's hideaway.

Diana turned on her heel. Her eyes were shining. She tucked her books tightly under her arm and set off at an athletic trot toward home.

Chief Mulcade's florid face looked a little bewildered. He sat behind his scratched mahogany desk and listened with a tired expression as his subordinate went on talking on the phone.

"All right," he said eventually. "I suppose I'd better see them."

He put the receiver down and straightened the pile of papers on the blotter in front of him. A heavily-built man of fifty-five, with close-cropped, dark hair, he had been Westchester's Chief of Police for ten years, and he was used to strange requests from residents of the wealthier sections of town. But this sounded strange even for Westchester.

His faded blue eyes looked tired above his heavy black mustache as he rose from the desk to greet the tall, lithe, dark girl who entered, followed by the young-looking, blond man.

"Miss Diana Palmer?" said the Chief cordially, coming forward to shake the girl's hand. "And this is your uncle; I already know Mr. David Palmer."

"Correct," said David Palmer with a worried smile. He took the pipe out of his mouth and pumped Mulcade's hand.

"What can I do for you?" said the Chief warily. "I thought the Desk Sergeant said something about pirates."

"So he did," broke in Diana excitedly. "That's why we wanted to see you."

Mulcade looked incredulous, but he did a good job of trying to hide it.

"Please sit down," he said, dragging two comfortable leather-backed chairs forward.

Despite his worried expression David Palmer gave a short laugh.

"Don't look so distressed," he said. "This isn't as fantastic as it sounds. And Diana, my niece, has a legitimate complaint to make."

"Ah, that's a different matter," said Mulcade, narrowing his eyes and looking interestedly from one to the other. "My job only demands investigation of crimes which were committed in this century!"

He joined in the laughter which followed.

"You look as if you could use some coffee," Mulcade said.

"That would be very nice," Diana said. "We came straight to you and I haven't had any dinner yet."

Mulcade looked at the clock. It was 10:30 p.m.

"I could have some sandwiches sent up," he said. "I think the emergency fund could stand it."

He lifted the phone and started barking instructions. Then he folded his arms and looked across at his visitors.

"Now, let's have it," he said.

"Well, have you heard about the research I'm doing at the University?" asked Diana.

Mulcade nodded.

"I caught the TV show," he said. "How does that tie in with a complaint?"

"I'm coming to that," Diana said patiently. "You remember I told the audience I had traced the Scorpia band to within 50 years of the present time?"

Mulcade nodded and settled back in his big chair.

"Well, tonight, just an hour ago, a man stopped me while I was walking home and told me to forget all about the Scorpia."

Chief Mulcade looked incredulous.

"A seventeenth century pirate band?" he said. "You must be joking."

Diana shook her head.

"I've never been more serious, Chief," she said. "He threatened me in no uncertain terms. Told me to give up digging into Scorpia's history."

"It's perfectly true. Chief," David Palmer put in. "The man said he was giving her his first and last warning."

"He did?" said Mulcade. "That's serious. What did he look like?"

He took down notes as Diana gave him the description.

"He was driving a dark Cadillac," the girl concluded. "I couldn't get the license number. It was too dark and besides he had his lights switched off."

"Driving without lights too," said Mulcade gloomily. "The list of offenses is mounting up."

David Palmer grinned as he belched sparks and smoke from his pipe.

"That's exceeding the permitted pollution level too while we're at it," Mulcade grunted, indicating the pipe.

"You'll be arresting us next," said Diana, laughing.

They broke off as a burly patrolman came in with a tray containing plates of sandwiches, a coffee pot, cups and saucers. He was so absorbed in looking at Diana that he almost missed his footing as he put the tray down. The Chief poured. When his two guests had started on the coffee and sandwiches he picked up the phone again.

"I'll get this description sent up to Records," he said. "They may know something. I'll also run a check on Scorpia."

"I'd feel a lot better if you did," Diana told him, putting down her coffee cup.

"We can't have people threatened like this in Westchester," Mulcade growled, spitting instructions into the phone. He put the instrument back onto its cradle and downed more coffee.

"How's the movie business, Dave?" he asked.

David Palmer scratched his chin thoughtfully.

"Sick, Jeremiah," he said, "but we scrape along."

The Chief nodded his head in sympathy.

"Yeah, guess you're right. Who's going *out* to see a bad movie when they can see a bad one right in their own home?"

His broad grin at David Palmer took the sting out of his words.

"All the same," the Chief mused. "It was a real occasion in the thirties when we stood in line for Gary Cooper and Shirley Temple. We won't see that again, unfortunately."

His nostalgic remarks were interrupted by the ringing of the phone. He picked it up briskly.

"Listening," he grunted. "Yeah, yeah. Got you. Well, keep at it."

He put the instrument down and sighed. He spread his hands wide on the blotter.

"We've got nothing in Records. No trace of anything called the Scorpia. We'll have to check with New York and Washington, of course, which will take time. And your blond man, Miss Palmer, doesn't match up with anyone known locally. We'll try and get some mug shots for you to look at. Apart from that, I'm sorry we can't be more helpful. Would you like me to put a watch on your house?"

David Palmer looked at Diana and then shook his head.

"I don't think that's necessary, Chief," he said. "But thanks just the same. We'd better be running along."

"If there's anything we can do, just give me a ring," Mulcade said.

Diana and her uncle walked down the steps of the police station and into the half-deserted street. The night wind listlessly flipped over the discarded cigarette packs in the gutter.

"Well, that didn't do much good," said Diana.

David Palmer shrugged. "You've got to admit it's difficult

from his point of view," he said. "What could the Chief do? Maybe he was right. It could be a crank."

Diana shook her head.

"This makes me more determined than ever to go on with my investigation," she said. "There must be something in this Scorpia business if it's important enough for me to be threatened."

David Palmer gave her a worried look.

"Listen, Diana," he said. "I'd forget this Scorpia business if I were you. I know how stubborn you are but consider the risks. And there's your mother to think of. It could be dangerous."

Diana compressed her lips into the firm line that David Palmer knew so well.

"I'm sorry, Uncle David," she said. "I must go on."

Neither of them noticed the blond man keenly watching them from the interior of a phone booth on the other side of the boulevard. He saw them pass the end of the street and then opened the door. He strode back up the sidewalk and turned off into a quiet, tree-lined avenue. A big Cadillac was parked in the moonlight. Cringle opened the door and got in. A cigarette lighter flared beside him, illuminating the flabby features of Otto Koch.

"Well?" he said softly.

Cringle looked frightened. He licked his lips.

"She ignored the warning," he said. "She went to the police."

CHAPTER 9

The Phone Man Cometh

The ringing of the front door bell brought Mrs. Palmer out of
the drawing room with a crease of annoyance on her normally
placid features. The housekeeper was out for the afternoon and
the houseboy, who usually attended to the door, was on vacation.
Mrs. Palmer herself had been working on an unusually elaborate
flower display on a table between the French windows, and so her
momentary loss of composure.

A tall man in the blue coveralls of the telephone company
was standing on the porch. He had a leather belt bristling with
pliers and other small tools strung around his hips, and carried
a metal toolbox in his hand. He raised his hand toward his smart
peaked cap in a semi-military salute as Mrs. Palmer opened the
door.

"Sorry to bother you, Ma'm" he said crisply. "I'm from the
phone company. We're doing our yearly wire check-up."

"Oh, I see," said Mrs. Palmer. She had two cut roses in one
hand and the clippers in the other, which was why she had had
difficulty in opening the door. She looked slightly bewildered.

"You'd better come in," she added, stepping aside. "Though I
don't know what you want to look at."

"Just leave it to me, Ma'm," said the tall man with a smile.
He took off his cap as he closed the door behind him, disclosing his

long blond hair. "It won't take more than half an hour."

"I hope not," said Mrs. Palmer. "I have to go out shopping shortly and I'll want to lock up the house before I leave."

The telephone man smiled faintly as though he'd heard it all before.

"There won't be any problems, Ma'm," he went on. "Or any mess. Just leave it to me."

Mrs. Palmer hovered in the hallway as the big man put down his toolbox. She was mollified to see that he first put a soft cloth on the tiles and then lowered the toolbox gently onto it.

"Isn't this something new?" she queried.

The repairman shook his head.

"No, Ma'm" he replied. "We've been doing it for years. It's a necessary routine."

"I see," said Mrs. Palmer.

Her somewhat severe expression softened.

"Perhaps you'd like a cup of coffee when you're finished. I plan to have a cup myself a little later."

"That would be fine, Ma'm. If you could just show me the main telephones in the house and any extensions I'll get on with the job."

"Certainly," said Mrs. Palmer.

She took the man around the house and showed him the phones. Then they went back to the hall. She watched for a moment, understanding little of the purpose of the instruments and meters he unloaded from the metal box. Presently, she grew tired of the performance and went back to the drawing room.

"I shall be in the next room if you need me," she said.

The telephone engineer nodded.

"Thanks very much," he said.

He went on humming softly to himself as he bent a piece of wire over with a pair of pliers and attached a meter to it with a metal tag. He concentrated on the needle on the dial, which started flickering to and fro.

Mrs. Palmer shook her head and went back to her roses. The house settled down to its customary afternoon quiet. Diana was away playing tennis with friends and David would not be back until six o'clock. She soon forgot the engineer's presence as she concentrated on the arrangement. Then the doorbell shrilled again. She went out into the hall to find the upholsterer she had expected. She noticed a trailing wire leading up the stairs, but the tools and the metal box had been cleared from the hall.

There were several more callers that afternoon, and by the time Mrs. Palmer remembered her promise to the repairman, nearly an hour had gone by. She hastily made the coffee and carried a tray into the hall as the big man came back down the stairs, dusting his hands.

"All is well, Ma'm," he said, accepting the cup she had poured.

"I replaced the wiring to one of the extensions, since it was frayed where it passed under one of the carpets in the upstairs hall."

He indicated a small coil of cut wire at his belt as he spoke.

"That's fine," Mrs. Palmer told him. "As long as everything works."

"Everything works just fine, Ma'm," said the big repairman. "And thanks for the coffee. It isn't something we get at every house."

"I should hope not," Mrs. Palmer laughed. "You'd never get your work done if you spent all day drinking coffee."

She gave the engineer a shrewd look.

"You're sure this is a free service, and you're not going to send me a bill for a couple of thousand dollars for rewiring?"

The big man shook his head as he put the cup back in his saucer with a smack of satisfaction.

"Nothing like that, Ma'm. Like I said, I'm from the phone company. Would you like to see my card?"

Mrs. Palmer refused the offer, smiling gently.

"Certainly not," she said. "I didn't doubt you for a minute. Besides, I've seen your truck outside. But one can't be too careful these days."

"Too true, Ma'm," the big man said.

He paused by the door.

"And thanks again."

The sunlight shone on his blond hair and for the first time, Mrs. Palmer became aware of a faint scar on the side of his face, which seemed to affect the lid of one eye.

Then he was gone and the door had closed behind him. Mrs. Palmer sighed as she looked at the hall clock. It would be too late to do her shopping now.

She cleared up the coffee things and went back to the drawing-room and the contented creativity of her flower-arranging.

Otto Koch's face looked impassive as someone knocked on the door of his private quarters.

"Who is it?" he asked.

His hand went as quickly as a snake to a drawer in the table at his elbow. He put the big Luger revolver down on the cushions of the couch at his side, where he could get at it in a second.

"Cringle," said the soft voice.

Koch grunted. He got up ponderously and crossed to the door with light steps. Once again, there was a marked contrast between his bulk and the lightness of his movements. He unlocked the door. Cringle stepped inside. He wore a raincoat over his clothing. On his head gleamed a peaked cap. He whipped it off with a grin and hurled it triumphantly across the room. It hit the couch and fell with a thump to the floor.

"I hope you didn't bungle it this time," said Otto softly.

Cringle smiled.

"It went like a dream, Chief," he said. He took off the raincoat disclosing blue coveralls, the knees of which were covered with dust. He brushed them absently as he went to put a metal toolbox down on the carpet.

Otto's grey eyes looked skeptical.

"You're sure this will work?" he asked. "Your wiring expertise hasn't gotten as rusty as your Morse?"

Cringle bared his teeth in a hard smile.

"You'll soon see, Otto," he said.

"Let's hope so, Cringle, let's hope so," Otto said.

He went to sit down on the couch again and picked up a crossword puzzle book he'd been working on when the other knocked. The thick ash from his cigar fell unnoticed onto his shirt.

"No one recognized you?"

He frowned at the puzzle.

"Two across, dumb pelican's lament," he said. "Back-breakingly difficult. I'd better leave that."

He shot a glance over the top of the newspaper at his subordinate.

"You took a chance going there after Diana Palmer had already seen you. I assume she wasn't there?"

"Certainly not, Chief," said Cringle in an aggrieved voice. He went to a hard-backed chair and sat down, taking a pack of cigarettes from the pocket of his coveralls.

"I checked it out first. Only Mrs. Palmer was home. She didn't suspect anything."

"Well, we shall soon find out," said Otto imperturbably. "When I've finished this puzzle, we'll go upstairs and turn the receiver on."

He smiled blandly at Cringle.

"If it fails to work, I shall personally punish you."

His eyelids went up and the full power of his gaze was directed toward the man with the scar.

"And you know what that means?"

Cringle shifted uneasily on the chair.

"Don't worry, Otto," he said. "I checked and double-checked. It will work."

"It better," Otto said. He went back to his crossword puzzle while Cringle smoked silently on.

Presently Koch threw the paper down with a curse.

"We'll be here all night," he said. "Let's see how good you are."

He led the way up to the attic. In the boarded room he sat down comfortably in his customary chair by the couch and waited for the blond man to complete his preparations. Cringle went to the bench and shifted his chair farther along, away from the Morse key.

He flipped a row of switches on the front of a grey-painted metal bank of receivers. He turned a dial, frowning in the dim light of the overhead lamps, his face a mask of concentration. A low hissing noise began to come out of the grill of the large loudspeaker on top of the bank of equipment

He turned to Koch with satisfaction.

"It's alive," he said. "I put a miniature microphone in every room of the house."

He grinned.

"Including the bathrooms."

Otto said nothing. He did not share Cringle's distorted sense of humor.

"I hear nothing," he said mildly.

Cringle smiled again.

"That's because I'm tuned into an empty bedroom," he said. "I wanted to make sure I was up to strength first."

He flipped another switch and the speaker went dead. Koch frowned. He opened his mouth as if to say something, then appeared to change his mind.

Cringle turned on another microphone. Mixed with the static, Koch could hear the faint rumble of traffic, the barking of a dog; somewhere feet were rat-tatting across a parquet floor.

"I got this one in the hall," said Cringle. "What did I tell you. A first-class job."

Koch grunted.

"What do you want, the Congressional Medal of Honor?" he demanded. "This is what I pay you for."

He sucked in his breath.

"For the money you get, Center expects first-class work."

He moved his chair nearer the speaker.

"What's happening?"

"Nothing right now," Cringle replied. "We won't hear anything until someone comes home. Diana Palmer's mother's alone in the house until early evening."

Koch glanced at his watch.

"It's nearly five-thirty," he said.

"If we don't get anything positive tonight, we'd better take turns listening in. It could take days."

Cringle suddenly sucked in his breath. He had heard a change in the sounds being monitored on the speaker. He fiddled with the dials, bringing up the volume. A loud hissing noise filled the loft. Then there came a loud bang that almost made Koch jump. Cringle hastily turned the volume control down. Koch realized the explosion had been the closing of a door.

A voice both men recognized boomed through the room. "Hello, Mama. Have a busy day?"

Cringle turned to Koch in triumph. He lowered the volume a little more to get rid of the distortion.

"That's Diana Palmer's voice," he said. "We hit the jackpot."

He fell silent as Koch's imperious forefinger quelled him. The speaker was full of sound again.

"Yes, a man from the phone company was here, the upholsterer called. There've been nothing but interruptions all afternoon. I didn't even get a chance to go shopping."

"Never mind," said Diana's voice. "I'll go out for you in the morning if you want me to."

Koch listened for an hour. It was an hour of small talk. He finally stood up.

"I'm going to get something to eat," he said. "I'll bring you some coffee."

Cringle nodded. He was evidently pleased with his toy. "I'll make a note if anything important happens," he said.

He flipped a row of switches and inclined his head toward the hissing speaker as the other man went out The door slammed heavily behind him.

Koch came back in half an hour with coffee and sandwiches. Cringle held up his hand for silence. He was scribbling rapidly on a pad. Diana Palmer's voice was coming through on the speaker.

"I've got more research to do tonight."

"Diana, I do wish you'd forget that Scorpia nonsense," said her mother.

"But Mama, I don't think it's nonsense," Diana replied.

"That's just it," said Mrs. Palmer's voice. "I don't like it at all. You've been warned. It may be dangerous to go on."

"But don't you see, Mother, that is just why I must go on," the girl replied. "There must be something in it. Otherwise, why would anyone want to stop my investigations?"

"Uncle David thinks it's a crank," Mrs. Palmer went on.

"In that case, it won't do any harm to complete my thesis," Diana said.

Otto's cigar burned steadily in his mouth as he fixed his grey eyes on the ceiling. He sat impassively, as though the conversation meant no more than a casual radio program he'd happened to tune into. The noise of the door slamming came through the loudspeaker. Cringle took the opportunity of the lull to pass his notes over to Koch. Otto studied them without saying anything.

David Palmer's voice was coming through the speaker now.

"You're still on that, Lily, are you?"

There was a brief silence, then his voice continued.

"The more I think about that Scorpia business, the more it baffles me."

"Me too, David," said Mrs. Palmer. "But it's frightening as well. I wish she wouldn't go on with this."

"You know Diana," said David Palmer.

"You're both the same, but you realize I've made up my mind," Diana went on.

"Maybe I'm on a wild-goose chase, but I intend to find out what Scorpia really is, Uncle Dave."

"Well, my dear, I'll back you in everything you want to do," said David Palmer. "But I think that it's simply an isolated crank trying to grab a little of your limelight."

"I'm not saying you're wrong, Uncle Dave," the girl answered. "But I've got to go on until I find the answer, or until I've proved that the entire business is nonsense."

"Well, there's obviously no more to be said," came Lily Palmer's voice.

"I think we've had enough of Scorpia for one evening. We'd better go into dinner, Diana, if you want to go down to the library later."

"I promise I won't talk any more about it—tonight," said Diana mischievously.

There was a burst of laughter on the speaker and then the faint sound of a door slamming.

Cringle turned off the switch and silence descended again.

"Well, that's it," he said to the silent walls. "She's obviously determined to go on with it. The girl's a nut."

Koch turned his strange grey eyes on his subordinate with that penetrating gaze that filled Cringle with such foreboding.

"Here, I strongly disagree with you, Cringle," Otto said. "This girl has courage, tenacity, resilience, many qualities you lack. Above all, she is highly educated and intelligent. The two do not necessarily go together. That is what makes her dangerous."

He bent over the message pad Cringle had given him and read the contents through once more.

A brief smile flickered across his plump face.

"So the Baron thinks the situation deserves only an Amber, does he?"

He looked sharply at Cringle, who brought his chair up

opposite the Morse key.

"Prepare another transmission to Center."

He smiled again as he bent over a signal pad, composing his message.

"And make it Red Alert!"

CHAPTER 10

The Baron Makes a Decision

Castle Toeplitz frowned above an azure sea. Baron Sojin stood staring intently out the great curved window until Colonel Crang began to feel that he had forgotten his presence. His silence was so profound that the ruler of Scorpia seemed oblivious to time and place. It was only when the Colonel coughed discreetly that he turned and came back to his desk.

Today he wore a sky blue uniform from the neck of which hung the blue Maltese cross of the Order of Scorpia, the highest honor the kingdom could bestow. Naturally, the Baron was the only man to hold it. Now his blue eyes looked even more startling beneath his short chestnut hair as he smiled his crooked smile at the commander of his security forces. He sat down at his desk and stared at the blank television screen that was turned like an eye toward him.

"So this Diana Palmer persists in her efforts to find out what Scorpia is?" he said.

Colonel Crang shifted uneasily from his position beside the great globe of the world on its mahogany stand. He glanced across at the Baron's disposition map, where little winking lights spelled out the nefarious activities of Scorpia all over the world.

"Koch was quite emphatic on that point, sir," he said crisply.

He glanced down again at the signal sheet in his hand.

"It seems that his Red Alert may have been correctly

designated this time."

Sojin smiled again.

"Perhaps," he said softly.

He drummed quietly on the surface of his desk with his thin, restless fingers.

"What is Diana Palmer like, apart from being an Olympic athlete and an explorer?"

He turned his gaze up to the bulky form of the Colonel.

"These are the only two things which the news bulletins seem to know about her. There must be more information."

"There is," Colonel Crang said quickly. "I have her picture here. We've built up quite a dossier on Miss Palmer."

He crossed to the end of the desk and picked up a brown leather briefcase that was lying there. He rummaged around in it, and then came up with a large envelope, emitting a grunt of satisfaction. He took a glossy photograph from it and passed it across to the ruler of Scorpia.

The Baron studied the studio portrait with great interest.

"She is beautiful," he said, involuntarily. He shot Crang an approving glance.

"I am obliged for this visual proof of the lady's charms. Colonel."

He turned back to examine the picture again.

"The face has courage, intelligence and tremendous personality," he said.

"Please sit down."

He indicated a leather armchair and Colonel Crang sank gratefully into it. He stared impassively at Sojin who continued to drink in the details of the picture. There was silence in the room for a long time. The faint hum of the air-conditioning seemed an intrusion.

Then Sojin slid the picture to one side.

"I'll keep this," he said.

His blue eyes were on the Colonel again.

"What would be your advice in these circumstances—as Chief of my security arrangements, of course?"

The Colonel leaned forward in the armchair.

"You want my frank opinion?"

Sojin spread his hands wide on the desk.

"Naturally, Colonel."

Crang frowned. He knew he had to speak cautiously at this stage.

"If I were in your position, sir, I would send Signal Black back to Koch," he said.

His words seemed to echo and linger unnaturally under the

great oak beams of the ceiling.

The Baron sat as impassive as a statue, his hands firm and relaxed on the blotter.

"Go on, Colonel."

"It would be the best way, sir," Crang went on.

"Within twenty-four hours Diana Palmer would have disappeared forever. Quietly and without a trace."

Sojin was silent for a moment. Then he smiled his crooked smile.

"Without a trace—and quietly—such a famous personality as Miss Palmer?"

He turned to study the picture again.

"An Olympic swimmer? An explorer? Oh, come now, Colonel Crang. You don't really mean what I think you mean."

Crang stirred uncomfortably in the chair.

"You make it sound difficult, sir."

The Baron inclined his head toward his Chief of Security.

"You have hit the exact point, Colonel. It is difficult."

He held the picture up to the light spilling in from the window.

"Don't you think the world press will make a fuss if Miss Palmer disappears? Not to mention television and the other news media?"

Colonel Crang coughed discreetly for the second time that afternoon.

"You have mistaken my meaning, sir. Perhaps my choice of the word 'disappear' was a clumsy one. But if Miss Palmer were to die . . ."

He lifted his stubby hands toward the silent figure of Baron Sojin at the desk before him.

"To die in a manner which suggested, unequivocally, that her death was an accident"

The words appeared to hover in the air between the two men.

"Then the world would have to accept the facts of her death as an 'accident,'" concluded the Colonel with quiet triumph.

The Baron put the picture down abruptly at his elbow.

"What other information do you have on Miss Palmer, Crang? I understood you to say there was a dossier."

"I have it here, sir."

Crang slid the folder across the desk to the Baron. He opened the cover with his thin, strong fingers and proceeded to examine its contents. Crang sat at ease in the chair, busy with his own thoughts. Half an hour passed without either man speaking. It was a silence compounded of mutual respect and trust. Finally, the Baron closed the folder with a grunt of satisfaction. He glanced at the picture again and put it in the folder with the other material.

"As I said, the girl has not only beauty, but brains and courage," he told Crang.

"An unusual combination in this modern age."

He got up and went to the window and stared moodily down at the panorama of cliff, sea and jungle. Crang watched him without expression.

The Baron turned to face him once more.

"She doesn't frighten easily," he said. "That is most unusual in itself. I don't care how you do it. Bring her here!"

Crang was on his feet, almost without knowing it. Dark blood suffused his cheeks as he replied.

"Do I understand you correctly, sir? We've never done anything like that before. Surely, it would be more politic to get rid of her quietly as I suggested?"

Baron Sojin's blue eyes were suddenly drilling into the Colonel's own. He lapsed into silence. An oppressive atmosphere seemed to have descended on the great room. Crang felt a rivulet of sweat run down his collar. He stood at attention.

"I prefer to believe that you did not make those remarks, Colonel Crang," said the Baron icily. "Do not let me have occasion to refer to it again."

He came up closer to the Colonel.

"You have your orders. See that they are carried out. Bring her here safely and without a scratch."

He crossed over to his desk and sat down on the edge of it.

"She's a pilot," he said. "I will dictate the method to be used. One that will convince the world of its genuineness."

"Very good, sir," said Crang crisply. "I await your instructions."

Once again he was a loyally functioning machine.

He saluted and went out

The Baron hardly heard him go. He reached over and opened up the folder. He studied the photograph for the third or fourth time.

"Brains, breeding and courage," he breathed to himself. "Things I've waited for for a long time ... all in one person, Diana Palmer."

He smiled his crooked smile. He felt strangely content.

CHAPTER 11

Night Kidnap

Rain was coming down steadily. Mrs. Palmer looked with surprise as Diana came to the drawing room door. She had on a white slicker and a head-scarf. Mrs. Palmer frowned. She put down the expensive, color volume on flower arranging and shook her head.

"You're surely not going out tonight, Diana? You haven't a class this evening."

Diana Palmer smiled. "No, that's true, Mama, but I thought I'd go down to the library for an hour or two. I'm taking a car."

"That's all right, then," said Mrs. Palmer, slightly mollified. "You'd certainly get drowned if you were walking."

She picked up the book, thought better of it and laid it on the couch beside her. She smiled at her daughter.

"I suppose there's no point in asking you to forget Scorpia for one evening?" she said gently.

Diana shook her head, but there were sparks of amusement in her eyes.

"Don't worry, Mama," she said, "This may come to an end sooner than you think."

Mrs. Palmer got up.

"Meaning what, dear?"

"Meaning that I'm getting frustrated," Diana replied. "I haven't uncovered a thing since my late nineteenth-century references to Scorpia."

"Maybe there isn't anything else to find, dear," said her mother. "Much as I hate to discourage you. . ."

She stopped, but Diana supplied the answer.

"You hope that there is no more to find out," she replied.

"I'm not saying you aren't right. It's just that I hate to leave any job half-finished."

"I know, dear."

Her mother bent forward to kiss Diana on the cheek.

"Have a good evening, anyway. Don't be late and don't get too wet."

"I won't, Mother," said Diana, walking across the hall and closing the door behind her. Once out of the shelter of the house, the wind buffeted her and she was glad to turn into the angle of the garage wing.

"Maybe there isn't anything else to find out about Scorpia," she told herself. "Maybe it's all my imagination."

Then her thoughts strayed to Kit Walker again, and she wished for the hundredth time that he were back in Westchester; he would know what to do in such a situation. She slid back the big doors of the garage and went around the bulk of the gleaming blue Mercedes toward the light-switch. She stopped with a shock of surprise as a harsh voice sounded from the darkness.

"Don't turn on that light, lady, unless you want to get hurt."

Diana whirled to find the dim form of a man in the interior of her car. The window was rolled down and the courtyard lights of the Palmer house, shining in through the open door of the garage disclosed the familiar hard face of the blond man Diana had seen before. He wore a dark raincoat and a dark hat, but the light from outside shone on the scar on the right-hand side of his face. It shone too, on the blue steel barrel of an automatic pistol which he trained unswervingly on her midriff.

"You're the man who stopped me on the street," gasped Diana. Her eyes widened. "You warned me off Scorpia!"

"That's right, Miss Palmer," the blond man said evenly. "Now just get in behind the wheel. Nice and slow or this just might go off."

Diana did as she was told. She now saw that the blond man was in the back seat of the car. He sat just behind her as she got in, and she stiffened as she felt the cold steel of the gun-muzzle against her face.

"Just take that head-scarf off, girlie, so I can see ahead," said the blond man.

"That's better," he said with satisfaction, sinking back on the seat.

"Now take her out nice and slow."

Diana felt the pressure of the muzzle relaxed from her neck.

"Do as I say and you won't get hurt," the blond man said as the engine throbbed into life.

"What did you mean about Scorpia?" Diana said, as she eased the car forward out into the rain. She bent to flip on the windshield wipers.

"No questions. Miss Palmer—just drive," the blond man replied.

The Mercedes whispered forward through the rain, along the driveway and out into the boulevard. As the headlights sliced across the drawing room windows, Mrs. Palmer craned forward with a smile on her face, straining her eyes to see into the dim light of the garden. Then the smile faded and was replaced by a frown.

"That's funny," Mrs. Palmer said, turning back into the comfort of the room behind her. "She usually flashes her headlights to me when she leaves. I wonder why she didn't this time?"

Diana turned left at the blond man's instructions. There were few other cars about in this section of Westchester, at this hour of the evening, and she made good time along the wet roads.

She turned her head briefly toward the man behind her, then contented herself with watching him in the mirror.

"Are you a member of the Scorpia?" she asked suddenly. "Does the pirate band that began in the seventeenth century still exist?"

The blond man smiled a sinister smile.

"No questions, I said. Just drive," he said harshly.

He scratched his forehead with the muzzle of the gun.

"A pistol in her back and she asks me history questions," he told the dripping trees as they fled past. Reluctant admiration showed on his face.

"You're quite a girl, Miss Palmer," he said.

"Never mind that," Diana told him. "This will cause a lot of worry to my mother and my uncle. I demand to know where you're taking me."

"You'll find out soon enough," the blond man replied. "Just turn off here."

The big Mercedes sent up cascades of water from its tires as the girl turned off onto a secondary road which wound its way through great shoulders of rock and slopes of scrub. She was silent, concentrating on the turns and the difficult terrain they were following. There were few houses along the way, and no lights broke the inky darkness. There was no sound except for the hiss of the rain and the faint throb of the motor.

The blond man relaxed, sitting slumped against the back seat, but Diana knew that he could send a slug crashing through the seat behind her before she could even try to escape. She decided to play safe.

It was more than an hour before her captor told her to turn again. Diana had not been able to read any of the sign-posts and she was now in country that was totally unfamiliar to her. The car rocked on through the night, over bumpy gravel roads. They went along for half an hour before the blond man spoke again.

"Take it easy, Miss Palmer," he said. "We're nearly there now."

"Where does 'there' mean?" asked Diana.

"A private airfield, Miss Palmer," her captor said. "You'll soon be out of the country."

He brought the pistol up threateningly, as the car lurched at Diana's reaction.

"Out of the country!" said Diana angrily. "It's impossible."

The blond man shook his head with a wry smile.

"Don't make trouble, Miss," he said warily.

"My instructions are to get you to the Center."

He gestured with the automatic.

"Through this gateway on the right and don't do anything foolish."

Diana nodded, holding back her angry thoughts. She steered the car gently over the undulating surface of the field, making for the yellow lights of a group of sheds. They were on paving now and the car traveled more smoothly. On the blond man's instructions, she brought the car to a stop near the largest of the buildings.

She got up, conscious of the barrel of the automatic near her back. They walked across the runway toward the dim shadow of a twin-engined executive aircraft. The engines roared into life as they approached. Diana bent down, the slipstream from the propellors whipping her hair and raincoat. The air door in the fuselage opened as they got closer, and a dark-haired man in a leather jacket looked out. Light from the cabin streamed across the runway.

"Up you go," said the blond man. "And *bon voyage!*"

He prodded her forward. There were two burly men in the cabin of the six-seater plane.

The pilot held open the door for her and then slammed and locked it. Below, the blond man moved away. The pilot was a big, chunky man with a thick black mustache. He grinned at the girl in a friendly manner.

"Don't be alarmed, Miss Palmer," he said. "Our orders are to treat you gently."

"That's nice of you!" said Diana sarcastically. She sat in one of the rear seats and strapped herself in. The second man sat across the aisle from her. Though he looked friendly too, he was even bigger than the pilot and she knew that even trained as she was in judo, she would have little chance against such a man, unless she caught him unaware. Her hopes faded as he casually produced a Browning revolver from the side pocket of his flying jacket. He grinned at her, showing strong white teeth.

"I don't want to have to use this, Miss," he said, tapping the revolver, then placing it on the seat beside him.

"You won't have to," Diana said as the engines revved up deafeningly. The cabin started to vibrate as the plane gained momentum. Soon it became airborne and its navigation lights faded into the immensity of the night.

It was nearly eleven when the phone rang in the Palmer household. Mrs. Palmer had the receiver off its cradle almost as soon as it rang. Relief sounded in her voice.

"Oh, thank goodness it's you, Diana. I was beginning to get a little worried. It's such a dreadful night."

"Sorry to upset you. Mama, I am over at Betty Hopper's and she asked me to spend the night. I hope you don't mind."

"Of course not, dear," said Mrs. Palmer. "It will do you good to get away from the library and your studies for one evening. What time shall I expect you tomorrow?"

"I thought I'd do a little flying in the morning, Mother. The field's quite near Betty's. It might help to blow the mental cobwebs away. I'll be home for lunch."

"That's fine," Mrs. Palmer said, looking relieved. "But do be careful, dear. If it's windy, like today, you shouldn't fly." "Don't worry, I won't. Mama. 'Bye.'"

There was a click as the connection broke. Mrs. Palmer sat back down on the couch. She lifted her book on flower arranging and consulted the index. But somehow she could not seem to relax. Twice she got up and went to the window. The wind seemed to rattle every shutter on the house and she could hear branches slapping against the roof. She had meant to get them cut back before. She would get it attended to as soon as the weather improved.

She fixed herself a martini and took it over near the fireplace. It was still only half-past eleven when the door slammed and her brother-in-law, David, came home. It had seemed a long evening without him.

CHAPTER 12

Lost at Sea

It was ten-thirty in the morning and a sparkling sun had dried the rain of the night when a blue Mercedes purred up to No. 4 hangar at McGuffey Field. The office of Charter Aircraft was crowded with pilots, and the roaring of engines seemed to make the hangars shudder as the field began to get up to peak activity. The dark-haired girl in the tailored raincoat drew the Mercedes up in front of the main administration building, locked it, and walked over to the office.

A man in a blue uniform and peaked cap gave her a friendly salute. The girl smiled.

"My name's Diana Palmer," she said. "I phoned about a charter this morning. Is it ready?"

"Certainly, Miss Palmer," said the officer. "If you'll just come into the office and sign the necessary papers."

He led the way into the administration office. A few hundred yards away the mechanics had noted the girl's arrival. The engines of a scarlet-painted, twin-engined, light aircraft were being warmed up as the officer and the girl came back down the steps. The blue-uniformed man saluted for the last time. He looked up at the sky approvingly.

"Have a nice flight, Miss Palmer. Wish I were going up myself, this afternoon."

The girl laughed.

"You fly nearly every day, Captain. For us amateurs, it means more."

The Captain laughed in his turn.

"You're hardly an amateur, Miss Palmer. Have a good trip."

He went off as the girl walked to the plane. She waved to the two mechanics and accepted the logbook one of them handed her. She went into the cabin, and closed and locked the door behind her. She got ground clearance from the tower and taxied down the apron, waiting for take-off clearance. The mechanics' eyes followed her in admiration.

"Was that Diana Palmer? I wish I'd had a better look at her. I watched her on T.V. when she took a crack at the record for the Polar Route."

The other nodded with approval.

"It's the first time I've seen her. She's one of the best women pilots around." Her clearance came through, and the scarlet monoplane gathered speed down the runway. It took off smoothly and turned westward, toward the sea. She dipped the plane's wings as she settled on course and the watching mechanics turned back to their work.

The first mechanic was climbing onto the wing of a constellation when he heard the voice of the officer who'd been talking to Diana Palmer.

"Briggs, would you mind going back to the office for me? I left my flight instructions there."

"Sure, Captain," said the man called Briggs. "Glad to."

He knew the Captain had an injured leg from the war and that walking up and down steep flights of stairs tired him.

The disability didn't show on the Captain's medical record, but Briggs was a close friend. Besides, the Captain knew he had his eye on one of the girls in the office. He grinned as he went up the staircase. A metallic voice came booming from the loudspeaker as he opened the door, and he listened in disbelief.

"This is AZEK ZEBRA 4210 calling McGuffey Control Emergency. Over water. Fuel starvation. Losing altitude rapidly."

The calm voice continued to give instrument readings. Everything except the aircraft's position.

The Chief Controller cut in on her transmission. He spoke crisply and to the point.

"What is your position, Miss Palmer," he said urgently. "Give us a bearing from the V.O.R."

The loudspeaker on the wall crackled back.

"I'm over water, and losing altitude rapidly. . ."

The Controller noticed Briggs at his elbow. He waved

him irritably away, but his expression changed as the mechanic whispered, "Miss Palmer can't be out of gas, sir. I tapped the tanks myself half an hour ago."

The controller checked the clock.

"She's only been up for ten minutes. It must be a mechanical failure.

The Controller nodded.

"Thanks, Briggs," he rapped. "We'll want your version later."

He addressed himself urgently to the mike.

"Please, Miss Palmer. Come in and report your position."

There was no reply except a faint static from the speaker. The men in the room looked at each other anxiously.

"Get search planes off," the Controller said, "and check coastal radar."

Far out over the Pacific, a scarlet plane dived against the azure blue of the sky. It flew over the white herringbone wake of a fast speed-boat heading seaward from the coast. Engines going at full throttle, it climbed back up to two thousand feet, then a parachute appeared against a fleecy formation of clouds, rocked in the slight breeze, the human figure beneath resembling a toy.

The scarlet fuselage of the plane glittered in the sunlight as it sped downward. It hit the sea at tremendous speed, an explosion followed, small and muffled against the immensity of the ocean. Then flame erupted amid the boiling spray, followed by acrid black smoke. The plume was visible for a long way before dissipating in the breeze. A few moments later, there was no visible sign of the plane's former existence, so swiftly had the ocean swallowed it.

The parachute grew larger now, and beneath it, the figure of a woman struggling a little as she fought to control the drift in the moderate wind. The sound of the speedboat's engine came across the sea and its bulk grew larger as it chopped through the waves half a mile away. The minute figure of the parachutist waved a greeting. Ten feet from the surface, she released the harness, and went cleanly into the water as the parachute collapsed and sank slowly into the sea.

The girl surfaced, swimming strongly and expertly toward the speed-boat, which was now only a hundred yards away. Her dark hair streamed behind her, then it too drifted away in the current. Freed of the wig, the girl's blond hair shone brilliantly in the sunshine. A man with a hard face reached down to grasp her wrists. With his help, she came aboard smoothly over the transom.

At the wheel, Otto Koch beamed, his bland priest's face exultant in the sunlight.

"Bull's eye," he said. "Well done, Vanessa!"

The girl smiled. She shivered suddenly and Cringle put a blanket around her shoulders. He thrust a cigarette between her lips and lit it for her.

"We'd better get out of here before the search planes come looking for Diana Palmer," he said, looking reflectively toward the coast.

"For once you talk sense, Cringle," said Otto calmly. "But just in case we should be spotted, get those lines out and try to look like a fisherman."

He looked at Vanessa again with approval.

"You'll find some whisky in the cabin," he said. "You did a first-class job."

The girl smiled a tight smile. She was obviously feeling the cold now.

"No more of this for me, thank you."

Koch smiled one of his rare sincere smiles.

"There won't be any more," he said.

CHAPTER 13

Drums For The Phantom

Diana Palmer drank the coffee gratefully as the co-pilot poured it. They had been flying steadily toward the east for many hours. She had lost all track of time. From the position of the sun she judged it must be well past noon.

"I suppose it's no use my asking where Center is?" she said.

The big man shook his head.

"You'll know soon enough, Miss Palmer. We're only the hired help."

He grinned, the light of the sun stencilling a dark bar of shadow across his face. He still had the Browning within reach. Diana took one of the sandwiches he offered her. She was hungry. Her mind was full of curiosity about the flight. It was not only her instinct for exploration but her love for flying itself which made the trip more bearable.

She looked curiously at the big co-pilot and asked a question that had been tantalizing her for hours.

"Why do you say I won't be missed?"

The co-pilot shrugged, his coffee halfway to his mouth.

"You just won't, that's all. It's not for me to explain. Hey, Clyde!"

He turned to address his remark to the pilot who had never moved during the entire flight, except when he turned to take food and coffee from the co-pilot.

"What?" he said crisply.

The co-pilot grinned.

"You're too inquisitive!" he said to Diana Palmer.

He turned back to the pilot.

"See if you can get WCRS on the radio. There should be a news bulletin coming on now."

The pilot nodded. He leaned forward and a moment later the whistle of static and then music filled the interior of the cabin. He twisted the dial and jazz replaced the first channel. Then he tuned in on WCRS. Bells tolled and an announcer's voice started giving the news of the day. After the usual static news of war and civil rights he got to local news.

Diana listened in temporary shock as she heard the even tones say, "The internationally-known Olympic athlete and explorer Diana Palmer was lost at sea earlier today when her twin-engined aircraft crashed on a pleasure flight. Miss Palmer, who won an Olympic gold medal for high-diving, was alone in the aircraft.

"Officials at McGuffey Airport said they could only attribute the accident to an unknown mechanical failure as the aircraft had been pre-flighted only half an hour before. Miss Palmer was an experienced pilot and had attempted a number of international records, including a Polar Flight three years ago. She had 1500 hours in the air.

"Despite an intensive search of the area by Coast Guard cutters and search planes, no trace of Miss Palmer or the aircraft has been found. Miss Palmer's mother, Mrs. Lily Palmer, refused comment on her daughter's disappearance."

The co-pilot reached over and flipped off the radio as Diana got up, spilling her coffee. The Browning was back in his hand.

"Easy, girlie," he breathed. "We don't want any trouble."

"You have convinced the world I'm dead," shouted Diana. "My mother and uncle must be going through hell right now. I've got to let them know I'm alive."

There was genuine regret in the co-pilot's eyes as he urged Diana back to her seat with an explicit movement of the pistol.

"Sorry, honey," he said. "No can do. I like breathing as well as you. Maybe you'll see your folks again. If you do as you're told."

Diana's fingernails bit into the palms of her hands as the plane droned on towards the coast.

The Phantom urged Hero through the jungle as the faint beat of drums came downwind toward them. The white horse whinnied eagerly at the sound and quickened his trot, picking his way with delicate precision through outcrops of rock. The noise of the drums receded and then became clearer as belts of jungle intervened. Steam rose from the ground at their feet and once Hero's hoofs were sucked into swampy terrain, before he turned off in response to the reins.

The big man's face was grim beneath the mask, and perspiration was staining his jerkin around the shoulders. There was something faintly sinister about the drums, something that he couldn't quite place. He was familiar with the rhythm of their messages and could read drum-talk reasonably well, but today, for some reason, the meaning of the hammered symbols eluded him. He was anxious to get to Skull Cave and he felt a sense of foreboding.

He had just passed through the waterfall when Guran met him. One look at the little man's face was enough to tell him that all was not well.

Guran's eyes were filled with tears.

"I hardly know how to begin, O Ghost Who Walks," he began.

The Phantom dismounted from Hero and bent to scratch Devil's ears affectionately as the great wolf rubbed his head against his legs.

"Just tell me the news, Guran," said The Phantom softly.

"It's Miss Palmer, O Great One," said the little man, speaking slowly and with great deliberation.

"She is missingl"

"How do you mean, missing?" The Phantom said.

The pygmy chief winced, as the big man's iron hand tightened on his arm.

"I'm sorry, Guran," The Phantom said, releasing him.

"Missing, O Great One, in an aircraft which has crashed into the sea," said the little man, massaging his upper arm gingerly.

"They do not know what happened."

Despite his shock, The Phantom quickly assumed control of himself.

"Missing," he repeated. "Not dead. There's still a chance."

He turned back to Guran.

"It doesn't sound reasonable. Diana is an experienced pilot. It is hardly feasible that she flew over the sea without checking the airplane carefully."

Guran shook his head.

"I do not know, O Ghost Who Walks," he said. "That is all that the Talking Drums said."

The Phantom was already walking rapidly to the entrance to Skull Cave, his brain working overtime as he made plans and evaluated possibilities. The little chief of the pygmies had a hard time keeping up.

"I shall be taking a long journey, Guran," The Phantom said as he strode down the tunnel leading to the interior. "I want you to take care of Hero and Devil while I'm gone."

The little brown man bowed.

"They will be treated just as though you were present, O Great One," he said gravely.

The Phantom took European clothes from a great carved chest in a corner. The torchlight flickered on his strong face as he turned to Guran.

"Send a message through to Colonel Weeks of the Jungle Patrol, Guran," he said. "I'd like a helicopter to pick me up. I must get to Mawitaan as soon as possible, from there I can pick up a jet to the United States."

The Bandar chiefs eyes were wide with compassion as he replied, "It shall be done within the hour."

As The Phantom changed into a lightweight suit and a collar and tie, only the set of his jaw and the expression of his eyes betrayed the pressure he was under.

"Was there anything else in the bulletins, Guran?" he said. "It would be useful to know."

Guran sat down on a stone ledge at the side of the cave and remained as though carved in stone for several minutes.

"I am trying hard," he said. "But I find your Western ways so difficult."

The Phantom smiled slightly, despite the seriousness of the situation. Devil went to sit opposite him and regarded him with great yellow eyes, as though he knew his master would soon go away.

"There was something," said Guran, eventually. "Miss Diana had evidently been in the news recently. She was studying something called the Scorpia."

"The Scorpia?"

The Phantom's eyes were sharp with interest. He finished knotting his tie and moved forward.

"Think, Guran! What else did you hear?"

The pygmy chief wrinkled his brows in concentration.

"It had something to do with pirates," he said. "That is all I can remember."

"Pirates!"

The Phantom's tone gave the word a wealth of incredulity.

"If Diana were studying Scorpia there must be some reason," he said. "She isn't a girl who would do research without hope of reward."

He straightened his jacket and buckled a pistol into a special shoulder harness beneath his armpit which did not disturb the line of his suit.

He led Guran along the corridor to the corner of Skull Cave where the records of four centuries of Phantom justice rested in great hardwood bookcases. Here, each Phantom had written the chronicles of his adventures in huge volumes bound in leather. The Phantom went to the massive carved wood lectern and consulted a register.

"Since we are interested in pirates, we had better start with the fifteenth century."

He turned back to Guran.

"You'd better get that message off or I won't get away today!"

"Certainly, O Great One!" said Guran.

He bowed and then scuttled away along the corridor, leaving The Phantom to the huge bound volumes and to the weight of his own thoughts. He carried the first of the tomes to the lectern and began the difficult task of deciphering the precise handwriting and archaic modes of expression. For the next hour he studied two of the great volumes and then an exclamation of satisfaction escaped his lips as he came across a reference to Scorpia.

His face was alive with interest when Guran came back two hours later.

"I've found some information about Scorpia," The Phantom told the little man. "They were a pirate band organized about four hundred years ago. My ancestors fought them through the years. They were almost destroyed but each time they returned."

The pygmy leader looked puzzled.

"This is beyond me, O Great One," he said helplessly.

"It's beyond me for the moment, Guran," said The Phantom. "But if Diana thought researching the Scorpia was important, then there must be something in it."

He sank his square chin into one massive hand as he went to sit at the lectern again.

"The Scorpia apparently died out in the late nineteenth century. What interest could they conceivably hold for Diana?"

Guran shook his head and transferred his weight from one foot to the other.

"Could Diana in her innocent research have stumbled onto something?" The Phantom went on.

"It's possible," Guran said, his brown eyes searching The Phantom's face with compassion.

"Anything is possible, Guran," said The Phantom, rising from the lectern and replacing the volumes on the shelves.

"I must leave soon. Thank you for your companionship during a difficult period."

The pygmy chief smiled with pleasure. The smile transformed his whole face.

"The Great One has thought of something?" he said.

The Phantom stood upright, the shadow of his great body enormous on the wall, reflected there by the light of the flickering torches.

"Diana is missing," he said decisively. "Missing only. There is a wealth of difference between being missing and dead."

He turned back to Guran, decisive and dynamic now.

"What time will the helicopter arrive?"

"Colonel Weeks said the machine will be landing near here within an hour. The pilot will take you wherever you want to go."

"Good," said The Phantom.

He folded a lightweight raincoat across his massive arm and picked up a dark brown grip from the ledge.

"Let's go then."

The two men walked to the entrance of Skull Cave, Devil bounding alongside. As they came to the entrance, The Phantom donned a great pair of curved, dark glasses which effectively shielded the upper half of his face. He pulled his white, panama hat down over his forehead.

"I rely on you to look after things here."

"All shall be as you wish, O Ghost Who Walks," said Guran solemnly.

The two men shook hands as the harsh beat of a helicopter motor sounded from the west and its shadow swept hugely across the jungle's carpet of green.

CHAPTER 14

Mid-Air Meeting

David Palmer frowned as the phone shrilled in the drawing room of his Westchester home. His face was beginning to show the strain of the last hours. He picked up the receiver irritably, and then his expression changed. The lines of worry seemed to smooth away a little as he listened to the faint voice of the long-distance operator.

"Mawitaan," he whispered to himself. "Then Kit Walker knows. He hasn't forgotten Diana."

He spoke into the mouthpiece, excitement blurring the edges of his voice.

"Yes, certainly. Of course, I'll hang on!"

Static and roaring noises and then, incredibly clear, that strong, calm voice.

"Mr. Palmer, is it true that Diana's been lost at sea?"

David Palmer took a firm grip on the receiver.

"I'm afraid so, Kit," he said. "Divers have found the plane. There was no trace of Diana."

There was a long silence at the other end of the phone.

"No trace at all?" said The Phantom slowly. "Do you think it was an accident?"

"Maybe," said David Palmer. "There's no proof at all that it was anything else. It could have been sabotage. Diana was threatened the night before she disappeared." He heard the faint intake of breath at the other end of the line.

"Threatened? What do you mean, Mr. Palmer?"

Diana's uncle hastened to explain.

"Something called the Scorpia," he said. "It was an ancient pirate band. She was doing research for her history term paper."

"Yes, I heard about that," The Phantom said. "But I didn't know that she'd been threatened. You called the police?"

"We went to them at once," David Palmer went on. "But of course we had nothing to go on. Diana's mother's taken it very badly. She's upstairs resting at the moment or she would have spoken to you herself."

"It's all right," The Phantom said gently. "I wouldn't want to bother her at a time like this anyway."

He paused again.

"I'm coming over right away, Mr. Palmer," The Phantom said. "I'll get to the bottom of this myself."

"We'll be glad for your help," David Palmer replied with relief. "What are your arrangements, so we'll be able to meet you?"

The Phantom gave him the plane schedules and then hung up.

Later that day, as the big jet lifted from Mawitaan International Airport, its shadow printed huge on the baking ground, The Phantom thought over the many possibilities. None of them made sense, but he felt that there had to be an explanation behind her disappearance. Somehow, he could not believe that the beautiful, dark-haired girl he had known and loved could be dead. He felt that there had to be an explanation behind her disappearance, that the end to their story was not an exploding aircraft sinking beneath the surface of the sea.

"The key is the Scorpia," he told himself, accepting the tray the air hostess placed in front of him as the big Pan-Am jet whined effortlessly forward, annihilating the miles between him and the U.S.A. Outwardly, he was an ordinary passenger, but inside, his analytical mind was unemotionally calculating endless schemes.

If Diana had found out something about the Scorpia, they might have wanted her out of the way. But would they knowingly destroy such a famous and distinguished person as Diana Palmer? Grimly, The Phantom had to admit to himself that they might, if the stakes were high enough. Such speculations could only end in complete mental fatigue before the end of his flight, so The Phantom outwardly calm, inwardly tense, forced himself to appear normal. He smilingly ate his meal and drank the coffee and then later, read The New York Times with such a concentrated look on his face that his fellow passengers never even suspected that his eyes absorbed nothing of what was printed on the paper.

He saw nothing, either, of the light aircraft which passed beneath the jet at a dangerously close distance. Up ahead in the Pan-Am cabin, the pilot gave a sharp exclamation as he saw the shadow flash across his vision and then disappear.

"Hell, Arnold," he said to the second pilot, a short, stocky New Yorker. "That wasn't on the plot. See if you can get Kennedy and give someone a roasting."

In the first-class passenger cabin, the stewardess had momentarily turned white at the near-miss. She bit her lip and then relaxed her mouth in a smile.

"Unusual to pass a plane so closely at sea, Sir," she said to the huge man in dark glasses who sat at a window seat.

The Phantom stirred.

"I'm afraid I didn't see it," he said.

"It was going east," said the stewardess. "Would you care to remove your hat, Sir."

"No thank you," said The Phantom.

He turned back toward the window as the plane whined on toward the west.

Diana Palmer gave a slight exclamation as the giant shadow of the jet sliced the air above them. The pilot swore and instinctively jerked the controls, though the danger was already past. Diana craned to rearward, but the big jet was now miles away.

"Our fault," said the big co-pilot with a grin. He had already done a stint at the controls and was piloting her again.

"One of the hazards of our type of operation."

Diana sank back on her seat again.

"Can't you tell me what this is all about now?" she said. "After all, you're safe. You're a long way from the States."

The big man's grin broke out below the thick mustache once again.

"All right, Miss Palmer," he said. "As you say, it's safe now. A woman using your name rented a plane. Then she radioed she was falling into the sea."

Diana gasped. Her mind had not yet grasped the implications.

"Actually, she parachuted down and we picked her up. As far as the world knows, Diana Palmer was on the plane. You are missing—almost certaintly dead, for the general public."

Diana gasped, "How could you do such a thing?"

"You ignored our warning," the co-pilot said calmly.

"You are the Scorpia!" said Diana indignantly.

The big man shifted on his seat and shrugged.

"A small part of it, yes."

"So, my hunch was right," Diana went on. "After four hundred years, the Scorpia band of pirates still exists?"

"In a somewhat changed form, but basically, you are correct," the big man replied.

Diana looked puzzled.

"But what do you expect to gain by kidnapping me in this way?"

The co-pilot turned a blank face to her.

"Ah, that's another story, Miss. Like I said, we're small cogs." He tapped his forehead.

"We don't know what goes on up there. That's where the brains are. Your guess is as good as mine as to why you're here. But you'll find out soon enough."

"What do you mean?" Diana asked.

"We'll be landing in five minutes," the pilot said unemotionally, banking the plane.

Blue sea and then jungle-clad, rocky island slid by beneath the wing-tip.

"We're almost there," said the co-pilot.

He picked up the pistol again and held it languidly in his right hand.

"Welcome to Scorpia, Miss Palmer."

"I may be dense, but I don't understand," said Diana, staring at him.

'This is the island of Scorpia, where the Scorpia organization has its Headquarters. You were curious about Scorpia, Miss Palmer."

He pointed downward. Diana saw a strange, turreted castle rearing from the great rock.

"You are looking at the Center!" the co-pilot said.

CHAPTER 15

The Phantom Investigates

D avid Palmer's face was somber with grief but it brightened as he spotted the huge form of "Kit Walker" coming down the staircase of the gleaming Pan-Am Jet. The Phantom's great fist engulfed his own as the two men shook hands. They were silent for a moment, the raucous noise of Customs' shed unnoticed. David Palmer had a special official dispensation to be in Customs. He rapidly explained what had happened to The Phantom as his baggage was being examined.

When they left the reception area, he said, "You came quickly. Thank God for that."

"As fast as I could, Dave," The Phantom replied. "How is Diana's mother?"

David Palmer frowned, taking The Phantom's suitcase as they threaded their way through the people in Customs.

"She's still in shock, I'm afraid. I can't believe it myself. I'm glad you came."

"I want to hear the whole story," The Phantom said as they reached the departure area.

"The car's over here," said David Palmer, leading the way to the parking lot.

"We don't know much," said David as they threaded their way to aisle 53.

"Never mind, Dave," said The Phantom. "Give me the facts in your own words, every detail. Any clue could be important."

Diana's uncle shot him an appraising look as they reached his car. He opened the door for The Phantom, put his bag on the back seat and then slid behind the wheel. As they joined the lines of cars leaving the airport area, he told his companion everything he knew. The Phantom listened in silence, his eyes invisible behind his sunglasses, nodding his head from time to time as Palmer emphasized a point.

David Palmer turned the wheel suddenly to avoid a truck that crossed without warning to another lane. He blew the horn and raised his voice, momentarily.

"Diana phoned to say she planned to fly in in the morning, and was spending the night with a friend."

He turned his troubled eyes toward the big man at his side.

"She'd never been near Betty Hopper's. We found that out afterwards. Lily said Diana's voice sounded strange."

"That figures," The Phantom said. "Her voice was obviously imitated by someone else and she'd already been kidnapped earlier that night. Anything else special?"

David Palmer frowned.

"Nothing special that I can think of. Lily told me about the call when I came in that evening, but it seemed to me that Lily suspected something was wrong. It wasn't like Diana to make sudden decisions to spend the night away from home. And then Lily said something else. . ."

He paused, waiting for the lights at an intersection to change. "Go on," The Phantom prompted.

David Palmer gunned the car ahead, turning off the crowded main highway onto a secondary road. Then they were making better time, as the built-up areas started thinning out.

"Well, it was something that Lily mentioned next day," he went on.

"Something about Diana not making her usual signal with the headlights when she drove out of the garage that evening."

The Phantom scratched his chin thoughtfully.

"We certainly haven't got much to sink our teeth into here, Dave," he said.

"What was the police's attitude?"

"Oh, like I said on the phone, they took it seriously, but it's difficult. There's so little to go on."

"Let's get back to the night Diana was threatened," The Phantom went on. "Diana gave you a description, you said."

"Yes," responded Palmer.

"She said he was a thin man with a hard face. He had long

blond hair which hung down below the brim of his hat, and he had a small scar on his right cheek, up near his eye."

"That sounds fairly distinctive," The Phantom said.

Palmer shook his head.

"One would think so, but the police had no luck. I saw Chief Mulcade again, after Diana disappeared and they'd come up with nothing in the files."

"Of course, the man might not have a record," The Phantom mused.

"Some crooks are fortunate for a while and aren't caught. But there's always a first time. Some other city may have a dossier."

"Oh, they're keeping at it," David Palmer said.

He looked sharply at his companion as he drove up the winding road through the hills. "You think the same man who threatened Diana kidnapped her?"

"It certainly looks that way," The Phantom said. "Those are the only threads we've got to go on. We can't afford to neglect any clues."

He shook his head.

"It beats me why she chose an ancient pirate band to research."

"That's the strange part," said David Palmer, turning the car off the road and onto another which was sign-posted: WESTCHESTER.

"She only became really interested after she read that The Phantom, your ancestor, had destroyed, or partially destroyed the Scorpia band in 1612."

The Phantom lowered his head. He looked unseeingly through the side window of the automobile.

"Strange and sad," he said gently.

Both men were silent until the car crunched through the gates of the Palmers' Westchester home.

After he had been up to see Mrs. Palmer, The Phantom sat for a long while meditating in his room. He had written notes on a number of points mentioned by David Palmer and he went over them again and again in his mind and on paper, sifting and re-sifting, trying to make some sense out of the tangled pattern of evidence.

Later in the evening, he went downstairs. He found David Palmer sitting in the study. For once, his pipe was not belching smoke and flame. David Palmer looked as though the heart had gone out of him. His pipe was empty and unlit, though still clenched between his square, strong teeth. He got up with a smile as The Phantom came in.

"Would you like a drink?" he said.

The Phantom shook his head.

"Never touch it," he said.

"Oh, I'm sorry, I forgot," said David Palmer, embarrassed. "Please forgive me. This business has been so upsetting. . ."

He broke off. The Phantom moved forward to sit opposite him.

"Nothing to forgive," he said. "I wondered whether you have Diana's research notes. I'd like to have a look at them."

"Certainly," David Palmer said. "I think she left them in the drawing room. I'll go and get them."

The Phantom sat absorbing the peace of the study with its dark, panelled walls until Diana's uncle returned.

He took the notebooks and loose sheets David handed him. He spent the next two hours opposite Palmer, studying the notes. Neither men said anything. David Palmer spent the time staring silently into the fire or playing solitaire in a half-hearted fashion. Eventually, The Phantom gathered the papers together with a grunt.

"Well, I've learned one thing," he said.

"What's that?" his companion asked.

"These notes indicate that Scorpia might still exist," the big man said. "I must learn a lot more, though, before I can be certain. I'm turning in now. Tomorrow I'll go to the airport and see what I can find out there."

The sun was shining brilliantly next morning when The Phantom drove David Palmer's car out to McGuffey Field. Today, he wore a tartan check raincoat with a silk scarf knotted at the throat. The dark glasses and low-slung fedora effectively masked the upper part of his face. A short while later, he came down the steps of the Administration Building with one of the senior executives.

"That's the man you want," the latter said, indicating a burly mechanic in the airfield's standard blue coveralls.

He introduced The Phantom.

"This is Mr. Walker, a friend of Miss Palmer's. He's making inquiries on behalf of the family. Please give him every assistance."

The mechanic turned a tough, good-natured face to The Phantom.

"Sure," he said. "Glad to oblige."

The two men shook hands.

"It was a terrible thing, Sir," said the mechanic. "I still don't understand how it could have happened."

"I believe you were one of the last people to see Miss Palmer before she took off?" the big man said.

The mechanic nodded.

"That's right. I serviced the aircraft. Everything was in A-1 order."

"I know," The Phantom said. "I've just looked at the check

lists. Nothing unusual there."

The two men were walking slowly across the apron now. The thundering reverberations of aircraft engines being started up echoed from the hangars further down. The Phantom turned his strong, broad face to the sun and gazed out across the runway from which Diana's plane had taken off.

"The gas tank was full?" he asked.

"I filled it and checked it myself," the mechanic said. He took off his long-peaked cap and scratched his unruly thatch of hair.

"She could not have run out unless a gas line broke. I heard her on the radio just before the plane went into the sea. She was quite calm. For some reason, she did not give a position report, although the controller asked for it"

The Phantom stood lost in thought for a moment

"Did you know Miss Palmer?"

The mechanic shook his head.

"I'd never seen her before. Naturally, I knew her reputation as a pilot. I followed all her record attempts."

He scuffed with the toe of his shoe on the rough surface of the apron.

"She didn't look the same as her pictures in the papers."

The Phantom made a sharp movement that startled his companion. He put his hand on the mechanic's arm.

"Say that again."

The mechanic looked puzzled.

"I thought she didn't look much like her pictures, that's all."

"No?" said The Phantom.

A faint suspicion of a smile was playing about his mouth.

"How do you mean?"

"She seemed so much younger and prettier in her pictures. She just looked different."

"Go on," said The Phantom. His face had relaxed now, but there was an air of alertness about his whole body, as though complex emotions were being held in check.

"I didn't really get a good look at her," the mechanic went on. "She wore dark sunglasses and a black beret pulled down over her forehead."

"Thanks very much," said The Phantom. "You've been a great help."

The mechanic took the folded bill The Phantom slipped into his palm as they shook hands; he put it slowly in the pocket of his coveralls.

"Thank you, very much," he said. "Glad to have been of service."

The Phantom drove rapidly back to the Palmer home. Dave

Palmer was cutting the front lawn, driving the big mower as though it were an automobile. He shut it off as the car crunched into the drive and rapidly crossed toward The Phantom.

"Any luck at the airfield?" he asked.

The Phantom slid out of the car and slammed the door behind him.

"It was an interesting morning," he said. He took the other by the arm and they went around the house to sit on a bench by the pool.

"I want to ask you something, Dave," he said. "Can you recall Diana ever wearing a beret?"

David Palmer shook his head.

"Not as far as I know. To the best of my knowledge, she never owned one, much less wore one."

The Phantom's face broke out in a smile. David Palmer stared in amazement.

"Just what I thought," The Phantom said.

"I've done a lot of figuring since last night and reached a number of interesting conclusions."

David Palmer got up and took a turn up and down the terrace. He came back to stand facing his guest.

"Just what do you mean, Kit?"

The Phantom passed a strong hand across his chin.

"I don't want to raise your hopes too much, Dave. And I certainly shouldn't say anything to Mrs. Palmer at this stage."

"Whatever you say," said David Palmer. His good-natured features wore a puzzled expression.

"I'm making a calculated guess that Diana is still alive," The Phantom said.

CHAPTER 16

A Guest at Castle Toeplitz

Diana Palmer stumbled up a rocky pathway on the Island of Scorpia, still feeling cramped from her long flight. Two men in loose-fitting denims and flat military caps walked with her. The black snouts of their Schmeisser machine guns were pointed at the ground as they carried them slung over their shoulders, but she knew they could swing them into firing position in less than a second.

In any case, even if she could escape, where could she go? For all she knew, Scorpia might be hundreds of miles from the mainland. Diana decided that she must remain calm and try to take advantage of any opportunity that might arise. She walked up a steep stone staircase hewn from rock. The castle of Toeplitz rose dizzily into the sky before her.

The two men with her stiffened to attention and saluted, as they got to a great arid space at the top of the steps, above which the castle gates rose. A huge man, with a massive head like a pineapple, saluted the two soldiers perfunctorily, and looked curiously at Diana. He wore a lightweight tropical uniform, and gold epaulettes glittered in the sunshine.

"I am Colonel Crang, Chief of Security at Castle Toeplitz," he told Diana. "Welcome to Scorpia."

The girl ignored the Colonel's outstretched hand.

"It would be more meaningful if you told me why I've been

brought here," she said curtly.

The Colonel gave a little bow.

"Ah, that is not for me to say, dear lady," he replied. "It is outside my sphere of authority. But you will know soon enough. And now, if you will accompany me . . ."

He dismissed the two soldiers, who saluted again and marched smartly across the baked rock parade ground toward the Castle gates. Diana and her escort followed at a more leisurely pace, the Colonel adjusting his Malacca swagger stick smartly beneath his arm.

Far above them, the sun reflected momentarily on something at one of the windows, radiating dazzling beams of light. Baron Sojin again raised the binoculars to his eyes with a satisfied smile. He focused the glasses impatiently. Then Diana's figure came into focus, tremendously magnified by the powerful instrument. The Baron smiled his thin smile.

"Even prettier than her pictures!" he exclaimed, involuntarily. He turned away from the window and went to a mirror at the far side of the great room and admired his image.

"Hurry, Colonel," he said softly. "You know I don't like to be kept waiting under such circumstances."

The elevator whined smoothly upward as Colonel Crang examined Diana Palmer carefully. Now that he had met the famous athlete he could well understand the Baron's interest. He felt a momentary twinge of envy. It was a lonely, celibate life out here. But all he said, with a bland expression, was, "This is Center, Miss Palmer. The Headquarters of the Scorpia, about which you have expressed so much interest."

The Baron's instructions had waived protocol today, so there were no security checks; no magnetic keys in locks; no images on television screens. Colonel Crang ushered Diana Palmer in through the tropical greenery and slid the door aside for her. He walked with the girl toward the Baron's desk. Baron Sojin rose as they approached.

"Miss Diana Palmer," said Colonel Crang gravely. He introduced the girl with a gesture of one massive hand, as though the Baron might not have noticed her.

He turned to the girl.

"This is Baron Sojin, ruler of Scorpia."

"Thank you, Colonel Crang," said Sojin, fixing the Colonel with steady eyes.

"You may withdraw. I shall ring if I require your services."

"Thank you, sir," said Colonel Crang.

He saluted the Baron smartly, gave a half-bow and a tight smile to the girl and went out. Diana and the Baron remained warily facing one another until the door closed behind the Chief of Security.

"Well, Miss Palmer," said the Baron at last. "This is a great moment. Do, please, be seated."

The girl stepped forward and sank gratefully into the padded chair indicated by the Baron. She still carried her handbag, raincoat and scarf and the Baron graciously relieved her of them. Then he went to the other side of his great desk and sat down again. He slid open a drawer and took out a buff-colored dossier. He opened it on the blotter before him and was silent for a moment or two. Diana said nothing.

Baron Sojin's mirthless smile was a true indication of the man's nature, thought Diana as the minutes ticked by. His face was not unpleasant until one came to the mouth.

"You were curious about Scorpia, Miss Palmer," he said at last. "Well, now you have met its leader and you are at present in it's headquarters."

He turned and pointed to a large, carved table that had been set for a meal, beyond his desk.

"But I forget my manners. You must be hungry after your long flight."

Diana spoke to the Baron for the first time.

"I'm not hungry," she burst out. "Why on earth have I been brought here?"

The Baron raised his hand soothingly.

"All in good time, my dear lady. And you *are* hungry. Why allow your prejudice to overcome your good sense?"

Diana was silent. She allowed the Baron to usher her forward. She felt faint suddenly as she reached the table. Sojin took her arm, and put a glass of wine in her hand.

"Drink this," he said. "You will feel better."

He lifted the silver dish covers from which came the rich aroma of finely cooked food. His eyes expressed amusement at her unspoken question.

"No, my dear Miss Palmer, it is not poisoned. Come, you must eat."

"What is Scorpia?" asked Diana, as she started eating. She had realized the Baron was right. It would be ridiculous to allow prejudice to overcome common sense. She would need all her strength for the tasks before her. The Baron watched with satisfaction as she ate and drank.

"Scorpia?" he said.

He pointed to the large, illuminated map of the world which occupied one side of the enormous chamber.

"That is Scorpia, my dear."

His hand made a graceful motion in the air.

"You will see we operate everywhere in the world."

"I see," said Diana non-commitally, putting down her wine glass and lifting another dish cover.

"But what does Scorpia do exactly? I know what it was in the Eighteenth Century, and I traced it as far as the late nineteenth. What is it now?"

The Baron's face lit up.

"Ah, there you have touched on something close to my heart, Miss Palmer."

He got up and started to walk around the room, a commanding figure in his immaculately-tailored blue uniform.

"As you so correctly observe, Miss Palmer, the Scorpia is an ancient pirate band whose history extends back over four hundred years. Now we are more modern. As you surmised, the Scorpia did not die out in the late nineteenth century. It lived on, like the Mafia and other secret societies that the world knows little about in the twentieth century. But Scorpia is a hundred times more powerful than any of these."

His face was an exultant mask of greed as he spoke, and Diana momentarily recoiled. Then the Baron resumed his pacing.

"A pirate band," he chuckled. "We dispensed with sea piracy long, long ago."

He turned back to Diana.

"If you have finished your meal, Miss Palmer, come and sit near the desk here where you can study the map as I talk. My explanations will then be clearer to you."

Diana got up and walked to the chair indicated by the Baron, her lithe steps drawing approving glances from the ruler of Scorpia. The Baron approached the great map with its glowing symbols. He surveyed it proudly.

"No, we no longer bother with sea piracy," he mused, half to himself. He turned back to the tall, dark-haired girl in the chair beside him.

"As I told you, our operations today are world-wide. They embrace smuggling, counterfeiting, gambling, protection rackets, bank and jewel robbery."

The Baron spread his hands apart, pride in his voice, as though he were describing the world-wide operations of a banking concern. Diana could hardly believe her ears.

"Of course, our operations also embrace other, less desirable activities, but we won't examine those too closely at this stage."

Diana tossed her head.

"I should hope not!" she said.

"That's right," said the Baron, as though his guest had agreed with him.

"Wherever an illegal dollar is to be made, Scorpia makes it."

Diana involuntarily stiffened in her chair.

"Scorpia then is nothing more than a world-wide crime ring?" she said.

"That's one way to put it," said the Baron smugly.

"Of course, we're unknown to most of the people who work for us. And we're also largely unknown to the outside world."

He went to sit opposite Diana at his desk and looked at her approvingly.

"We're the hidden power behind criminal groups in a dozen nations," he said. "And we've got such extensive power that we almost control some countries."

Diana forced herself to remain cool and outwardly unconcerned.

"How did Scorpia become so powerful?" she asked.

There was genuine curiosity in her voice.

The Baron was silent for a long minute. His speech had a strange timbre, as he replied.

"Time, Miss Palmer. Purely time. Centuries of time."

He got up again and went to stand by the map, as though his physical presence enabled him to exert personal power over the Scorpia agents in all parts of the globe.

"I am the tenth generation of my family to rule Scorpia, Miss Palmer," he said simply.

He looked musingly at the girl.

"Do you realize, Miss Palmer, that we hadn't been mentioned in print for over fifty years until you decided to write a thesis about us?"

A tiny spot of red showed on the cheek Diana had turned toward the ruler of Scorpia.

"I knew nothing about your modern activities," she said. "I thought Scorpia was a band of ancient pirates."

"You were doing research," the Baron interrupted smoothly. "Research which could have led you to the fact that Scorpia is not extinct."

He looked up at the great glowing map on the wall behind him.

"Your research was attracting considerable publicity because—unfortunately, for you—you are a celebrity."

His voice had dropped until it was now no more than a whisper. The effect was most sinister. Diana realized that she was in the presence of a very dangerous man.

"Is that why you brought me here?" said Diana with a sudden intake of breath.

"One reason," replied the Baron. "We dislike people

investigating Scorpia. We stop them. Sometimes violently."

He paused imperceptibly.

"There was another reason, Miss Palmer."

"Yes," said Diana, shifting in her chair.

"What was that, Baron?"

Baron Sojin smiled his dead smile. He bowed toward her slightly as he spoke.

"I admired your picture. That is why you are here."

CHAPTER 17

Missing Link

Sunlight shimmered on the surface of the Palmer swimming pool, the brilliant reflection making The Phantom contract his eyes slightly despite the dark glasses he wore. It reminded him vividly of the pools of his jungle home in Bangalla and of Guran, Hero and Devil. He and David Palmer sat on a bench alongside the pool. Ever since The Phantom's revelation of his thoughts to David on his return from the airfield, Diana's uncle had recovered something of his old manner. His pipe was belching smoke and flame again as he listened to his companion's reasoned arguments.

"That's all very well, Kit," he said in answer to a specific point. "But we've no real proof that Scorpia still exists or plotted to kidnap Diana."

"Perfectly true, Dave," said The Phantom, resting his strong chin on his hands.

"Neither the police nor the F.B.I. have any record of Scorpia."

He raised his eyes from the pool and looked squarely at his companion.

"It was a well-planned operation. If Scorpia took Diana, their plot was perfect. The plane accident at sea was ingenious."

He shook his head and continued to look at the sparkle of the sun on the water. His demeanor was so rigid and strange that David Palmer looked at him in surprise.

"Their plan was perfect," repeated The Phantom softly to himself.

He snapped his fingers and rose abruptly. He brushed against Palmer, almost knocking the other's pipe from his mouth.

"It was too perfect, Dave!" said The Phantom raising his voice, oblivious to his startled companion. He went pounding across the patio toward the house. David Palmer sprinted behind him in bewilderment.

"What's happening?" he called.

The Phantom turned his head without decreasing his speed.

"If Scorpia planned to kidnap Diana, they'd have to have known her every move," he said. "Down to the most minute detail."

He vaulted over a low hedge that ran alongside the terrace. His footsteps echoed from the tile as he rushed through the French doors. A Japanese gardener who was pruning a bush in front of the house fled in terror at the sight of the gigantic man charging past him.

David Palmer was only a few yards behind. He found The Phantom pacing animatedly up and down the drawing room.

"There's just one missing link, Dave," he said as the other came into the room. "If we can only find it!"

"You've lost me," said Dave Palmer, sinking down on a couch and fiddling with his pipe. He looked around vaguely for his pipe-cleaner.

"How about an explanation."

"Don't worry," said The Phantom. "I'll explain everything, later. Just let me work out my hunch. I don't want to upset Diana's mother. Can you make sure we won't be disturbed?"

"Certainly," said David Palmer. He went out and gave instructions to one of the servants. When he came back three minutes later, he was astonished to see the huge form of his guest on hands and knees probing behind the draperies and under the carpet.

His face was a mask of utter bewilderment as The Phantom said in a loud, clear voice, "It's such a lovely day, Dave, I think it would be nice to take a stroll outside."

"But we've only just come in," mumbled Palmer, conscious that things were rapidly sliding beyond his comprehension.

He found his arm seized in a vise-like grip. He hardly touched the ground as The Phantom dragged him back toward the French doors. A thin chain of sparks from his pipe danced in the air behind him. But The Phantom had his finger to his lips and a warning look in his eyes.

The two men walked in silence down the drive.

"I'm sorry about that, Dave," said The Phantom when the house was well behind them. "But I couldn't explain in there. I had to make sure we were outside first."

"What on earth's going on?" said his bewildered host.

"Every room in your house is bugged!" said The Phantom.

David Palmer's eyes widened even further.

"All the rooms have hidden microphones," The Phantom went on. "Scorpia has been listening in. That's obviously how they were able to kidnap Diana. They knew where she was going and where she'd be every minute of the day."

David Palmer was belching smoke furiously from his pipe. His eyes had an angry expression.

"A man came to check the wiring the day before Diana disappeared," he said.

"That's the answer!" said The Phantom excitedly. "Now we know. It means that Scorpia exists. They took Diana. Now to find them!"

Palmer shook his head sadly.

"They took her, Kit," he said slowly, "or killed her."

"There's one way to find out," said The Phantom simply. "That is, if Scorpia is still listening in."

"I don't quite follow you," said Palmer.

The two men were walking back to the house now.

"What do you want me to do?"

"Just listen and play along with my conversation," said The Phantom. "I'm going to put on an act. You just keep replying normally to my lines."

They went back across the terrace and re-entered the drawing room. The Phantom made an unnecessarily loud noise in re-fastening the French windows behind him.

"This new evidence the police have dug up should be decisive," he said, winking at Palmer. "With what I've just learned it gives us a clear picture."

Palmer nodded, conscious of the bugging device hidden away somewhere in the room.

"How will you find Scorpia?" he asked.

His voice sounded unnatural and stilted to his own ears, but he was encouraged by The Phantom's ready smile.

"I've several leads to Scorpia," The Phantom said. "I'm going to take them to the police tomorrow."

"But are you sure Scorpia exists?" Palmer asked.

"No doubt about it," said his gigantic companion decisively. "That's definite. I know who they are and where they are."

He stopped talking and crossed the carpet softly, sitting down next to Palmer on the couch. He put his mouth to the other's ear, his voice the merest whisper so that the microphones had no chance of picking it up.

"I'm sure these microphones are still alive," he said. "They would need to know the household's reaction to Diana's disappearance. If they are monitoring, I'm sure they'll do something—fast."

David Palmer nodded. His pipe was belching smoke and flame as he puffed furiously, his face a reddened mask as it reflected the glowing bowl of the pipe.

The two men stiffened as the strident ring of the phone broke the silence of the room.

CHAPTER 18

Scorpia Calling

Diana Palmer's face was puzzled.
"You brought me here because of my picture?" she asked the Baron.

They were sitting on a long steel and leather divan that faced the largest and most spectacular window in Castle Toeplitz. Below them the fiery ball of the sun was being extinguished in the steaming rim of the sea. The sky was blood-red, and the gigantic crimson vision tinged her face and that of the Baron with carmine. They momentarily assumed the aspect of some satanic scene from the Castle's long and brutal history.

Baron Sojin smiled his mirthless smile.

"It was a lovely picture," he said. "But not as beautiful as the original, Diana."

The girl blushed and shifted uneasily on her end of the couch.

"That's nonsense!" she said.

Her eyes expressed contempt.

"My mother and uncle think I'm dead at sea! I insist on getting in touch with them at once."

The Baron slowly shook his head.

"I'm afraid that's quite impossible. I am offering you something far more important."

"What do you mean?" said Diana.

"A unique honor," the Baron replied, leaning across the couch toward her.

"A new life, no less. You are being promoted from Miss Palmer to Queen of Scorpia!"

Otto Koch's eyes expressed infinite satisfaction as he sat in the attic room watching Cringle taking down his daily message from Center. He noted that the message did not have top priority, and he waited for Cringle to decipher it, the ash from his cigar dropping unheeded on the front of his suit. He glanced at the message when it was completed.

"Routine," he said, handing it back to Cringle. "File it."

He stood up, a bland and yet deadly figure, and went to stand in the next bay.

"I suppose we'd better listen to the monitor tapes," he told his associate. "And find out what the Palmer household's up to."

Cringle went over to switch on the big, multi-channel tape recorder.

Koch listened intently. The playback machine had an electronic device which by-passed the tedious hours of tape when there was nothing being recorded. So the two men heard nothing but the actual conversations taking place at the Palmer home. This saved wearisome hours of listening.

Cringle stared incredulously as he adjusted the volume of the recording. The voice boomed through the attic.

"But, Kit, are you sure Scorpia exists," came David Palmer's voice.

"Certainly," said The Phantom. "I know who they are and where they are."

Koch's cigar fell from his mouth and showered sparks as it rolled across the room. He ignored it. A quick twist of his wrist and Cringle had adjusted the controls. When they had finished the conversation, Cringle re-wound the tape and they listened again.

Cringle blinked and passed a tongue across lips which had suddenly become dry as he saw the expression in Koch's eyes. The bald man gestured again.

"Get the Palmer home on the phone," he said softly.

Cringle found his hands trembling as he leafed through the book.

The Phantom had picked up the receiver almost as soon as the phone rang. He listened to the voice at the other end for a moment and then said, "My name's Walker. Who are you?"

"Never mind who I am," said the voice. "You have information about Scorpia?"

"That's correct," said The Phantom.

He motioned to David Palmer who tiptoed to the other end of the drawing room and quietly picked up the extension. The Phantom could see him taking notes as the conversation went on.

"We want to know about Scorpia too," the mystery voice went on. "We'll pay well. Are you interested?"

The Phantom smiled thinly.

"How much?" he said crisply.

"Name your own price," the voice said. "Let's meet and talk it over."

"All right," The Phantom replied. "I take it you're not anxious for publicity and that you won't want to come here?"

There was a dry chuckle on the line.

"That's perfectly true, Mr. Walker. I like discretion. How about midnight tonight?"

"That's a bit sinister, isn't it?" The Phantom went on. "Not to say corny."

The chuckle sounded again. "That's the way we operate. We couldn't live without melodrama."

The Phantom chuckled in his turn.

"All right," he said again. "Where?"

"Don't worry," the voice went on. "It'll be a public place. You know the big stone wall opposite the Museum? We'll meet there. See you tonight, Mr. Walker."

There was a click and the phone went dead.

The Phantom found David Palmer back at his side. His pipe was belching smoke and flame furiously and there was a transformed look on his face.

"Don't worry, Dave," said The Phantom, laying a hand on the other's arm. "We've got our first big lead now. We'll just have to sweat it out until midnight."

"Who is this Walker?" said Cringle. "And what do you make of all this?"

Otto Koch sat on the couch and smiled.

"They must have found our microphones. They're trying to trap us."

He smiled again.

"They must think we're idiots to fall for their scheme," he said slowly.

He turned his piercing grey eyes on Cringle in the way that the latter found so disconcerting.

"What would you do in my place, Cringle?"

The blond man made no reply for a moment. Then he looked up, the lamplight glinting on the scar on the side of his face. He patted the .38 caliber pistol he took from his pocket significantly.

"Exactly my sentiments," said Otto with satisfaction.
"I am glad that we are in agreement."
He lit up another of his interminable cigars.
"We'll meet Mr. Walker tonight," he said softly.

CHAPTER 19

Rendezvous at Midnight

Midnight was chiming from the big clock in the tower of the Museum buildings when Cringle drove the Cadillac through the last intersection and along the side of the complex.

"Shouldn't we have radioed Center?" he said nervously.

"I'll handle this myself," Koch said shortly. "We can radio Center afterwards, when we've done the job. My standing orders are to stop all mention of Scorpia anywhere. It's a basic policy."

Cringle nodded. He turned the car down a side alley and stopped alongside a big wall of granite which rose up under thickly clothed trees. It was quiet and secluded, and ideal for their purposes. He drew in his breath with a hiss. There was a low stone parapet opposite and beyond that, the trimly cut lawns fronting the Museum. A big figure in a belted raincoat, with a dark fedora pulled down over his eyes, was sitting casually on the wall, with his feet on the grass.

"There he is," Cringle said. He turned the car in a sudden U, raising the headlight beams to illuminate the man better. They drove slowly back, Cringle slowing the big car to a walking pace.

"Mr. Walker," Koch called softly.

"Here," the big man replied. "Are you Scorpia?"

"Yes!" said Koch decisively.

The rattle of the sub-machine gun in Koch's hands seemed to slap Cringle's eardrums with physical violence. Flame lanced from the muzzle and was answered with sparks from the wall. Stone chips flew angrily into the air as Koch stitched across the sidewalk, the bullets moving upward, flaying the wall. The figure of the big man disappeared suddenly, punched from his perch with shocking violence. The stench of cordite filled the interior of the Cadillac. It was like perfume to Cringle.

"Not bad, Otto," he said. "Congratulations."

"We'd better make sure," Koch said. "Mr. Walker has had his payment from Scorpia."

He smiled. He and Cringle got out of the car, leaving the engine running. They vaulted over the wall. Cringle was the first to reach the crumpled figure. He turned it over.

"A dummy!" he said disgustedly.

Koch whirled too late as an enormous figure launched itself over the wall. A revolver glistened in his hand.

"I'm here for our appointment, Scorpia!" said The Phantom in ringing tones.

Koch snapped up the tommy-gun too late. There was a thin crack and flame bloomed in the darkness of the Museum grounds. Koch felt a numbing pain in his fingers, and the weapon fell to the grass. The Phantom pushed the two men back and picked it up.

"Back to the car," he said. "The whole town will be here in a moment."

A few seconds later, the Cadillac roared off into the night. A solitary patrolman rushed up just in time to see the taillight disappearing in the direction of the main street. He noted the bullet marks on the sidewalk and across the wall. He vaulted over and inspected the clothing gingerly. Then he scratched his head.

"Clothes with some busted balloons inside!" he said. "What the hell gives here?"

He went up the street at a fast pace, looking for the nearest police phone.

The Phantom sat at ease in the back of the Cadillac, his pistol trained steadily on the back of Otto Koch's head.

Otto sat with a handkerchief tied around his injured hand, his whole arm aching. There was a dull ache of rage in his brain at being outwitted. Cringle drove normally, but the whiteness of his knuckles on the steering wheel betrayed his tension. Now he looked in the mirror, astonished at the extraordinary being who had outsmarted them.

The huge man in the tight-fitting jerkin and hood laughed. A black mask covered the upper part of his face, so that Koch could not make out his features. He had a broad, strong jaw and square teeth which glinted as he smiled; which he was doing right now. Koch took a quick hold on himself.

"Are you Mr. Walker?" he asked softly.

He half-turned in his seat, stiffened as he felt the muzzle of the pistol against his cheek.

"How did you. . .?" Koch went on.

"Where's Diana Palmer?" The Phantom interrupted him.

"Diana Palmer's dead," Cringle answered, turning his head furtively.

"Shut up, fool," said Koch, something of his old manner returning. "We know no one of that name."

Cringle seemed to cringe in his seat.

"I meant I read about her in the papers," he said. "She was a pilot."

He watched The Phantom carefully in the big rear mirror.

"You're both lying!" The Phantom snapped.

"Drive me to Scorpia Headquarters."

Otto Koch drew himself up and put his pudgy hands in his lap.

"Mr. Walker, you can shoot us," he said slowly. "But it won't get you any closer to Headquarters."

The Phantom could see tiny beads of sweat running down Koch's forehead as his face was reflected in the mirror.

"We have an ancient law in Scorpia," Koch said. "That is, die before revealing information!"

He smiled bitterly.

"Stop the car here," said The Phantom. They had reached a lonely spot outside the town, where a ravine ran alongside the road. The Cadillac slid to a halt and Cringle cut the motor. Both men turned around to look curiously at The Phantom, who leaned calmly back, holding the revolver steadily where both men could see it clearly.

"What do you know of the history of Scorpia?" he asked.

"Shooting us won't get you to our hideout, Mr. Walker," Cringle said.

The Phantom laughed.

"Mr. Walker isn't my name. It's short for the Ghost Who Walks. Does that mean anything to you?"

Otto Koch started and his face turned pale. He glanced quickly at Cringle.

"The Ghost Who Walks is The Phantom," he gasped. "The legend says that he fought the Scorpia centuries ago!"

He turned back to the big man in the rear seat. His eyes were hard again.

"Are you trying to tell us you're that Phantom? A ghost? Do you think we're idiots?"

He snorted. "I've read about the skull mark. It's a lot of rubbish."

His fingertips at last touched the butt of the Luger strapped to the leather upholstery at his feet. He brought the gun up, turning with triumph on his face. The Phantom's mighty fist came up with the force of a sledgehammer. There was a tremendous crack as it caught Otto Koch beneath the chin. His head slammed back against the window frame and he sagged unconscious, a thin trickle of blood running from the corner of his mouth. The gun dropped to the floor of the Cadillac.

"I don't think you need that," said The Phantom calmly. To Cringle, he added, "Pick it up!"

Sweating with fear, Cringle bent slowly and searched for the Luger with his fingertips. One look at The Phantom's set features told him not to try anything. He handed the gun to the big man, butt first, and felt it taken from him. He stiffened, his eyes focused on Otto Koch's unconscious face. The mark of a skull was grinning up at him from the unconscious man's livid flesh!

"The skull!" he gasped, looking at The Phantom with sudden fear on his face. "Just as the legend says! Who are you?"

"I told you," The Phantom answered imperturbably. The pistol muzzle remained trained unwaveringly on Cringle's head.

"Now drive me to your hideout."

Cringle swallowed heavily. Sweat ran down his face.

"We will die before revealing our Headquarters," he said in a quavering voice.

"Very well," said The Phantom inflexibly. He advanced the pistol until its cold rim seemed to be eating into the blond man's neck.

"You will obey the ancient law!"

Cringle gave a muffled cry as he heard a minute click behind him. His nerve broke. He twisted away.

"All right!" he said. "I'll take you there. The law will have to be broken this time."

He put the Cadillac in gear and the big machine moved forward through the night. Otto Koch was groaning his way back to consciousness as Cringle pulled up in front of the farmhouse and switched off the engine.

Koch struggled up, massaging his jaw tenderly with one pudgy hand. All his self-confidence seemed to have deserted him.

"Fool!" he snarled to his companion. "Why did you bring him here? You know the law of Scorpia!"

Cringle turned a twisted face to him.

"Just look at yourself!" he said. "That's why!"

Puzzled, Koch turned to the rear-view mirror and examined his face carefully. He began to tremble as the reddened skull symbol stamped into his puffy flesh stared back at him. He got out a handkerchief and passed it across his face, as though the action would erase the mark.

"The sign of The Phantom!" he stammered. "I don't understand."

"You will," said The Phantom calmly. "Get out of the car."

The two men preceded The Phantom up the steps, their hands clasped behind their heads.

"Now, take me to your companions," said The Phantom when Cringle had opened the door and they were in the musty hall. "And no unnecessary movements, or this gun might just go off."

"We ought to go up normally, or they'll know something's wrong," Cringle said. Koch gave a low mumble of anger.

"That's all very well," Cringle flared. "But getting shot isn't going to help Scorpia."

"We will take this up later, clown," said Koch, with a flash of his former confidence.

The two men walked slowly up the stairs to Koch's private quarters. The Phantom swiftly searched the rooms while the two men sat on the couch and watched him sullenly.

"You must have a transmitter here somewhere," said The Phantom. "Where is it?"

"Up top," said Cringle, before Koch could reply.

The Phantom smiled.

"After you, gentlemen."

Cringle led the way to the attic room. As they got near the door, The Phantom's heart leaped in his throat. He could hear Diana Palmer's voice coming through the thin partition that separated them.

Diana was saying, "I must find out if Scorpia really exists."

Then another woman's voice broke in.

"Now listen," it went on. "I'll bet you can't tell my voice from Diana Palmer's."

The Phantom relaxed. He jammed the pistol in Otto Koch's ribs as the three of them stood listening outside the boarded attic room.

"I must find out if Scorpia really exists," Diana's voice repeated.

"That was great, Vanessa," said a man's voice enthusiastically.

The Phantom didn't wait for more. His mighty hand with all his weight behind it propelled the two men violently forward. There was a crashing impact and Koch and Cringle sprawled through the door and landed in a heap on the floor of the radio room. A tall, attractive blond turned with a start of surprise. Behind her, a rat-faced little man reached for a pistol on the bench beside him.

The Phantom seemed to fill the whole room with his

powerful personality as he leaned against the door jamb.

"I wouldn't touch that, sonny," he told the rat-faced man pleasantly. "Or you'll look like a Swiss cheese."

The rat-faced man trembled slightly and then withdrew his hand from the pistol.

The Phantom surveyed the cowering group with satisfaction. "You did a great job, Vanessa!" he said.

CHAPTER 20

The Ghost Who Walks

The blond girl called Vanessa goggled with surprise as she surveyed The Phantom; the black boots, the gun belt, the striped shorts and the hooded jerkin. The mask caused her the most amazement. She sat down on a chair near the rat-faced man and shook her head.

"Are you looking for a masquerade party, Mister?" she said.

The Phantom laughed.

"No, Vanessa. For a missing link! You imitated Diana Palmer's voice on the phone. You pretended to be her when you dumped the plane into the sea after parachuting out. "Now, where is Diana?"

The girl drew herself up and looked coolly at the big man with the strange garb.

"If you're so brilliant and know so much, you should know that answer too," she said levelly.

She looked contemptuously at the dusty forms of Cringle and Koch on the floor. Koch had certainly lost his image. He had hit his head in falling and his shirt was now covered with blood, as well as cigarette ash. The girl raised her gaze from the two men on the floor to The Phantom.

"If I did know where she was, do you think I'd tell you . . ."

She started back as The Phantom's pistol made a deafening roar in the confines of the loft. Through the blue smoke swirling in the air, the little rat-faced man screamed with pain. He looked stupidly at the scarlet patch on his shoulder as he went down. The pistol skidded from his nerveless hand and went skidding along the floor.

"I warned you, sonny," The Phantom said pleasantly.

He turned to the girl.

"You'd better look after him. And kick the gun over here."

The girl did as she was told. She helped the little man to a chair and plugged his wound with a handkerchief. Cringle and Koch had decided to stay on the floor. The Phantom picked up the pistol and broke it. He took out the slugs and put them in his pocket. He threw the gun into a corner.

"Perhaps I can find out where Diana is, without your help," he said levelly.

He crossed over to some filing cabinets in the corner and riffled through the documents.

"Like all efficient organizations, Scorpia keeps records," he said, as though to himself. He smiled suddenly.

"Ah, radio transcriptions."

He stared at the decoded signal pad. One phrase stood out: "BRING DIANA PALMER TO CENTER." He read it again and put it in the pouch on his belt. He crossed to a map in the corner. All the lines from various parts of the globe intersected at one point

"So this is your Center," he said interestedly.

The girl Vanessa rose from attending to the little man's wound.

"We operate in every country in the world," she said contemptuously. "Do you think you can fight us?"

The Phantom admired her spirit even as Cringle said sullenly, "He isn't a man! He's the Ghost Who Walks . . ."

The girl turned round.

"What does that mean?" she said.

They were suddenly interrupted by an incoming radio transmission. Cringle quickly went over and tuned in properly, prompted by The Phantom's pistol muzzle.

"Center calling, Center calling," said a man's voice from the metal-grilled speaker.

The Phantom whispered a few sentences to Cringle and then turned to survey everyone in the room.

"Sit down," he told them. When they'd obeyed, he turned back to Cringle.

"Stay close to me," he said.

Center was still requesting acknowledgment. The Phantom picked up the microphone.

"Calling Center," he said. "Calling Center. Westchester here.

Come in Center."

He watched Cringle switch to receive and waited tensely. The speaker was silent for a few seconds and then a voice boomed, "Are there any developments in the Palmer case?"

The Phantom pressed the switch on his microphone.

"Nothing to report," he said. "All quiet this end. How is Miss Palmer?"

The unknown operator at the other end was back in a few seconds.

"All right, I guess. They don't let me in on the top-secret information. What's your next move?"

The Phantom looked urgently at Cringle who moved quickly to his side and whispered something.

"Our instructions are to do nothing, but to keep the Palmer household under surveillance," The Phantom replied.

"That's good," the speaker crackled. There was a long silence broken only by the rustle of static. The Phantom thought he'd detected a slight quality of indecision in the voice from Center. His gun muzzle passed in a menacing arc across the three men and the girl in the room.

The man at the other end was speaking again.

"I don't recognize your voice," it said.

"I don't recognize yours, either," The Phantom said.

"Who are you," said the loudspeaker.

There was a note of urgency in the voice now.

The Phanton smiled as he switched over to send.

"This is The Ghost Who Walks!"

Baron Sojin's eyes widened with pleasure as he saw the effect his words had on Diana Palmer. The girl had gone to stand at the great window. She stood silent now, looking at the last of the sun reflected on the sea.

"You must look at things from my viewpoint, Diana," he said. "When you trumpeted Scorpia's name over television, we were naturally alarmed."

He crossed to the table where they had dined and lit a Russian cigarette from the silver candelabra.

"We, of Scorpia, dislike publicity. I decided you could be dangerous. Usually, when a person is dangerous to Scorpia, he, or she, quietly disappears. But then I saw your photograph . . ."

His voice dropped to a soft monotone and Diana could see his blood-red reflection in the window.

"Scorpia has always had a Queen," said Sojin simply. "I've chosen you, Diana."

The girl turned, her eyes widening, her figure stiff. Sojin held up his hand suddenly.

"Hear me out," he said. "Come over here and sit down."

The girl went to sit once more in the leather chair by this strange man's desk. Her eyes never left his face as he went on outlining the history of Scorpia and its place in the modern world.

Sojin tapped his cigarette against a crystal ash tray and leaned back behind the desk.

"The Kings of Scorpia in the past have often taken their Queens from Royal houses," he said. "They were my ancestors. Today, I am King of Scorpia."

Diana's eyes flashed.

"But today, Scorpia is only a gang of criminals," she said, witheringly.

Sojin smiled slowly.

"You expect me to marry you?" Diana continued. "To be Queen of the earth's human residue!"

"That's not a nice way to put it," the Baron said in the same, soft voice.

"It's the truth!" the girl replied.

"Very well then—Queen of criminals," the Baron conceded. "World-wide Scorpia."

"My answer to that is—no!" said Diana with great emphasis. "Send me home."

"My answer in turn must be no," Sojin retorted, a reluctant smile of admiration on his face. "But I respect your courage."

He went over toward the door and turned.

"That's why I chose you," he said with his dead smile. "I am young. I am patient. I can wait. There is no hurry."

Then his face softened as he looked at Diana's dejected form, slumped in the chair.

"You should consider it an honor to marry the hereditary King of Scorpia."

"It is a pleasure I must decline," Diana said in a muffled voice.

Sojin opened the door and prepared to step through into the adjoining room.

"Just remember, the world thinks you're dead," he added in a level tone. "You will never leave here, Diana."

The closing of the door sounded like a knell to the girl as it cut off the sight of the unyielding figure of the Baron. She put her head in her hands.

"What an impossible, hopeless nightmare," she told herself.

Sojin dropped swiftly downward in the elevator. The guards saluted as he walked across to the radio room. The Lieutenant in charge of Communications snapped him a smart salute as he walked in.

"Did you get hold of Westchester?" Sojin asked.

The Lieutenant nodded, a frown on his face.

"Yes, sir," he said. "The operator says that the person who answered must be drunk. All he would say was that he was The Ghost Who Walks!"

Sojin stiffened. He thrust his jaw out in a way the Lieutenant knew well as his vivid blue eyes transfixed the officer.

"Which one of our men was it?" he snapped.

"We don't know, sir," said the Lieutenant. "The voice was unfamiliar."

Sojin stood for a moment in quiet reflection.

"Perhaps it's some sort of current American slang," he said. "I'll ask Miss Palmer. Stand by for further orders!"

He clattered out of the radio room and rushed back to his apartment.

He found the girl closely examining the great illuminated map on the wall. She turned as he came toward her.

"I forgot to tell you, there's a self-contained suite for you up these stairs," Sojin said. "It can be locked from the inside, so you're quite safe."

"Thank you," Diana replied stiffly. "I am rather tired."

"Before you go," Sojin answered. "There's a little problem I'd like your help on. What does 'The Ghost Who Walks' mean?"

He was staggered at the girl's reaction.

Diana's face lit up in a dazzling smile.

"He found me!" she said.

"What are you talking about?" said Sojin curtly.

Diana threw her head back triumphantly.

"He saw through all your schemes! He knows I'm alive!"

Sojin crossed to his desk and sat down. His knuckles showed white on the desk before him.

"Diana, I don't know what you're talking about," he said, in a voice he was struggling to keep under control. "Would you please explain?"

"Certainly, Baron," the girl said in a cool, amused voice. She went to sit opposite the ruler of Scorpia.

"You've told me all about the history of Scorpia. Have you ever heard of The Phantom?"

"What's that got to do with The Ghost Who Walks?" said Sojin. His face was a mask of puzzlement.

"They're one and the same person," Diana said. "That's all the information I'm going to give you. Figure the rest out for yourself."

The Baron's feet clattered on the staircase. He reached a gallery where all the Archives of Scorpia were stored. He took several volumes from the shelves. When he returned in half an hour, the puzzled look was still on his face.

"I've looked up The Phantom," he said. "It's just an old legend, a myth."

"He may be a myth to you but he's very real to me, and he knows I'm alive," Diana retorted.

The Baron took a step forward. He put the leather-bound volume he carried down on the desk.

"Who is the Ghost Who Walks?" he said.

"I'll tell you nothing!" Diana snapped. "Ask that worldwide organization of yours. And now, if you'll excuse me, I'll say good-night."

"Good-night, Diana," said Sojin, absently. "I hope you'll find your apartment comfortable."

He waited until the girl had disappeared up the stairs and then he picked up the phone on his desk.

"Get me the radio room," he ordered.

"Carson here, sir," said the Lieutenant in charge of Communications.

"Carson, I want a radio tie-in to this telephone," said the Baron.

"I want to speak to Otto Koch in person. There's a lot of nonsense going on and I want to get to the bottom of it"

"Yes, sir," Carson gulped. "Shall I call Colonel Crang?"

"If I wanted Colonel Crang, I would have asked for him," said Sojin patiently.

There was a dangerous edge to his voice and Carson gulped.

"Sorry, sir," he said. "I'll try to get through immediately."

"See that you do," Sojin said.

He put the receiver in place and leaned back. His smile was not pleasant to see in the light of the match which illuminated his face as he lit another Russian cigarette.

CHAPTER 21

An Old Man Remembers

The Phantom's pistol pointed steadily at Otto Koch as the loudspeaker boomed again.

"This is Center calling. Is Otto Koch there?"

Koch's face was white and the skull symbol where The Phantom had hit him stood out vividly on his jaw. He had caked blood on his forehead to add to his sorry appearance.

He moved sullenly over and picked up the mike at The Phantom's whispered instructions.

"Koch speaking," he said.

The Phantom stood over him, holding the pistol menacingly. Koch licked his lips and flipped the transmitter switch. There were fear and pain in his grey eyes.

"This is Baron Sojin," the speaker boomed.

The Phantom shot an interrogatory glance at Koch. The plump man turned white.

"At your service, Sir!" he replied.

"I want a straight answer," the Baron went on. "Who was it who came on the air and said he was The Ghost Who Walks?"

The Phantom's gun-muzzle dug into Koch's ribs. The fat man groaned. Perspiration ran in rivulets down his flabby cheeks.

"Nobody, sir," he said in what he hoped was a normal voice. "I've been here all the time, Sir. I don't know what you mean."

"All right, there must be some mistake, Otto," the speaker boomed. "Thank you and good-night."

"Good-night, sir," said Otto with relief. He put down the mike and mopped his forehead with his handkerchief.

There was a clatter of feet on the stairs. The people in the room turned as the door burst open. The room was suddenly full of men in blue. Chief Mulcade's eyes popped as he caught sight of The Phantom in his costume. David Palmer was behind him, his pipe belching smoke.

"We got your message, Kit," he said. "Good show!"

Mulcade looked around the room in amazement.

"Who are these people?" he said, turning to The Phantom.

"The local branch of Scorpia!" said the big man with a grin, turning over their guns to a sergeant at Mulcade's elbow. He led the Chief of Police over to the filing cabinets in the corner of the room.

"They're a world-wide crime ring. I can't go into the details now. You'll find everything you need there."

He turned as David Palmer came up.

"Incredible," the blond man said. "You're amazing!"

The Phantom smiled at his enthusiasm.

"I'll need to be a lot more incredible before we have Diana back," he said.

"The important thing is that she's alive. I must get to her at once."

He pointed to the spot where all the lines intersected on Otto Koch's map.

"She's there!"

Mulcade was barking instructions to his men. Half a dozen burly officers led Koch and his subordinates away.

"We'll make out the charges later," Mulcade called. He grinned at The Phantom.

"Great job, Mr. Walker," he said. "We're indebted to you!"

"Temporarily, there must be no news leaks."

"Scorpia Center mustn't suspect we know their location."

He drew the Chief over into one corner of the room.

"Post some of your best men here from now on. Keep Cringle here so he can handle the radio. Then we can monitor all the messages from Center. It may give us more information."

The Phantom went over to the door. There was dynamic energy etched in every line of his body.

"Now, I need a plane—fast—at once!" he said.

Chief Mulcade turned admiringly to David Palmer as The Phantom's footsteps clattered on the stairs.

"Dave, who did you say he was?"

David Palmer grinned as his pipe erupted smoke and ash into the air like a miniature Vesuvius.

"You'd never believe me if I told you."

The radio operator's face was white. He stared blankly at Baron Sojin, inwardly shrinking at the icy contempt in his eyes.

"Either you were drunk or dreaming," the Baron said coldly. "Ghost Who Walks indeed."

He turned to Lieutenant Carson.

"Lieutenant, I am holding you personally responsible for this idiocy. We shall discuss it later."

"Yes, sir!" said the Lieutenant. He saluted stiffly, clicking his heels together. He looked viciously at the radio operator.

"Perhaps it was a misdirected message bounced off the ionisphere," said the miserable soldier. "I know I didn't imagine it."

"Silence!" the Lieutenant snapped imperiously.

He had to take it out on someone. He, too, would have a talk with the man later. He escorted the Baron to the door, expressing his regrets at the mix-up.

The Baron went out with a strange expression in his steel-blue eyes. He paused on the battlements. The tropical night had already fallen, but the overhead lights, adding their brilliance to the moon's radiance, lit the courtyard as though it were day. One could hear the faint swish of leaves from beyond the corner of a buttress. The Baron walked toward the parapet, his faint footfalls masked by the tinkle of an ornamental fountain. He found an ancient gardener raking up leaves from the base of a tree which grew from one of the diagonal flower beds. He stood for a moment, admiring the old man's energy and manual dexterity.

"Miki," he called softly.

The old man put his hand to the tip of his broad-brimmed hat and shuffled toward him. He took off the hat and twisted it nervously in his hands. The faded, brown eyes in the wrinkled, brown face looked anxiously at the ruler of Scorpia.

"Yes, Excellency?" he queried.

"Miki," said the Baron. "I want to ask you something."

"Anything, Excellency," stammered the old man. "I am eager to be of service."

"I know that, Miki," said Sojin softly. "You are the oldest living member of Scorpia."

"That is correct, Excellency," said the old handyman, with pride lighting up his face.

Sojin's face was grim beneath the glare of the lamps as he fixed Miki with an unwavering stare.

"Have you ever heard of The Phantom?" he said.

The old man started. He shifted his feet nervously on the cobbles of the courtyard.

"Yes, Excellency," he said in a low voice. "The Ghost Who Walks!"

Sojin was amazed but there was no visible change in his expression.

"Did you ever see The Phantom?" he next asked.

The old man shook his head.

"No, sir," he replied. "When I was a boy, my grandfather told me of the days when he was young."

He smiled suddenly and unexpectedly.

"My grandfather was a cabin boy when Scorpia *was* Scorpia. One night The Phantom came—The Ghost Who Walks. He blew up the ship's powder magazine. It was said he hated pirates."

Baron Sojin shivered suddenly at the slight breeze which had sprung up in the courtyard. His eyes seemed to have become clouded and filmy.

"Your grandfather actually saw The Phantom?" he said sharply.

"Yes, sir," said old Miki. "In those days, all who sailed the seven seas had heard of him. He was called the destroyer of piracy."

The oldster shook his head.

"He was four centuries old then," he said with wonder in his voice. "He is the man who cannot die. The Ghost Who Walks!"

Baron Sojin suddenly broke away from the old man with what seemed to be a definite physical effort.

"Thank you, Miki," he said, dismissing the handyman. "That will be all."

He walked over to the battlements and stared unseeingly out at the ceaseless murmur of the ocean.

"These old fools with their childish superstitions," he told himself.

He dabbed carefully at his forehead with his handkerchief. A chill seemed suddenly to have settled in his bones. He tried to throw off a sense of foreboding. That was what came of listening to old men's fantasies, he told himself angrily.

On sudden impulse, he went back to the radio room again. The startled face of Lieutenant Carson greeted him as he opened the door.

"I hope nothing else is wrong, sir?" said Carson nervously.

"Of course not," snapped the Baron angrily. He was beginning to lose control. He must watch himself. It was unlike him to suffer from nerves. He forced himself to smile in what he considered to be an amiable manner.

"I'd like you to contact Westchester again. Just routine, but I want to make sure of something."

"Certainly, sir," said Carson. "Will you wait here?"

"Of course I'll wait here," said Sojin, some of the savage edge creeping back into his voice.

He waited impatiently while the operator established contact. He got out his cigarette case and drummed his fingers nervously on its edge. He almost jumped when Cringle's voice boomed through the loudspeaker.

"Cringle replying to Center. Everything normal, sir. Do you have special instructions?"

Sojin shook his head. Carson took up the microphone. "Routine check," he told Cringle. "Everything normal. Over and out"

He put down the mike as the operator signed off. Baron Sojin was thinking hard as he rode up in his express elevator. He went through the big room with the magnificent views, extinguishing the lights. He tip-toed up the stairs to the gallery, hesitating outside Diana's door. Then he went to his own quarters. He was to have a very disturbed night.

CHAPTER 22

The Phantom Drops In

The jet droned on through the night. The hum of its motors made a smooth background to the thoughts of the pilot. And he had a lot to think about. He was a tall, broad-shouldered man of about thirty-five, with thick, black hair showing beneath his airline cap. Headphones were clamped over his head as he listened to a weather report. He reached forward to the instrument panel, and adjusted the squelch control.

"Roger," he said briefly. "Avoiding edge of storm area."

He banked the plane slightly, watching the compass, and settled down on the new course. He looked over curiously at his companion in the co-pilot's seat. The stranger had not spoken more than twice since the flight began.

The Phantom's face was frowning with concentration. Every minute was carrying him nearer to Diana. He wished he could double the plane's speed. Conscious of the pilot's eyes on him, he smiled in a friendly manner.

"We'll be over the island in about two hours, Mr. Walker," the pilot said. "I hope you're enjoying the flight."

"Everything's o.k.," The Phantom answered. "I'm not myself today."

"I understand, sir," said the pilot, while glancing at his instruments.

"I get all sorts of assignments, but this is one of the strangest. I can't help being curious."

The Phantom nodded.

"I wish I could tell you more," he said. "But unfortunately, my mission is top secret."

The pilot looked across at his companion and once again, wondered at the thick black boots, the mask and what he was sure was the bulge of a holster under the white belted raincoat the big man was wearing. Still, as the Airport Controller had said, it was none of his business. He noted the strong jaw, the set of the mouth and the resolve in the eyes. He wouldn't like to be on the receiving end of this man's displeasure.

"I'd really like to ask you why you're wearing that outfit, Mr. Walker," he said.

The Phantom chuckled.

"You've already asked, Captain," he said. "And I'd really like to tell you." He smiled again. "Curiosity makes the world go 'round."

With that the Captain had to be content. An hour and a half later, he alerted The Phantom.

"You'd better be getting ready," he said. "Would you mind sending the co-pilot forward."

"A pleasure," the big man assured him.

When the co-pilot joined the Captain, only half-awake, they gaped at their passenger. He was wearing his jungle clothes and with the parchutes strapped on, he looked even more impressive.

The co-pilot was wide-awake now.

"Excuse me, sir, but would you mind telling me why you're dressed like that?" he said, indicating The Phantom's striped shorts and the jerkin which joined a hood, hiding most of the big man's face.

"Your colleague just asked me that," The Phantom replied. "My answer is the same. It's top secret."

The pilot interrupted.

"There's the island dead ahead," he said.

The Phantom felt an increase in his pulse as he made out the dark form of an island rearing from the moonlight-splashed water. He discerned the sharp, turreted mass of what looked like a medieval castle.

"Can you drop me somewhere near that fortress but not within sight?" he asked.

"Can do," the pilot nodded. "I don't want to drop you in the jungle. I think I see an open space beyond."

"Fine," the big man grunted. He was already working his way aft to where the co-pilot had the cargo hatch open. Icy air whipped at him as he waited to jump. He waved as the pilot shouted, "Good luck, sir!"

He knew the Captain was watching him in the cabin

surveillance mirror.

"Good luck, sir," the co-pilot repeated, patting his back. "I'd still like to know why you're dressed like that."

The Phantom grinned.

"Tell you later," he said.

He nodded as the pilot turned on the jump light and the co-pilot tapped him on the shoulder.

He fell wide of the aircraft as it banked steeply to starboard. He fell free for 40 seconds then pulled the ripcord. There was a tremendous jerk on his legs as the chute opened. Then he rocked gently through the air, the great canopy of dacron above him shimmering faintly in the light of the moon. The ground came closer.

The big transport banked and circled dipping its wings in salute. Then it turned to the west and he was alone in the sky. The Phantom pulled in shrouds and sideslipped the chute. He landed perfectly in a small open clearing.

Baron Sojin was having a restless night. He turned feverishly in his sleep and unpleasant dreams kept tugging at the edges of his consciousness. The dreams included gigantic men who blew up pirate ships and ghosts who couldn't die. He groaned and then suddenly awakened. He switched on the bedside lamp, blinking in the sudden glare. His pajamas were drenched in perspiration. He looked at the clock. It was two a.m. Baron Sojin sat up in bed. Then he made up his mind.

He swung out of bed and donned his blue and white, striped bathrobe. He went to the bathroom and looked in the mirror. He sponged his face in the basin, combed his hair and then felt better. He returned to the bedroom and pressed a bell on his bedside table. He lit a Russian cigarette as he waited for his valet. The man's sleep-sodden features appeared round the door about five minutes later.

"Wake Miss Palmer," said Sojin, peremptorily. "Ask her to meet me in my study at once."

The man blinked as though the light in the room were too strong for his eyes.

"Yes, Excellency," he mumbled.

He went along the corridor to the secondary suite while the Baron made his way down the staircase. He was at his desk studying notes when Diana came down. She was wearing a pale blue negligee which enhanced her symmetrical figure and her magnificent black hair floated behind her as she came into the room.

"Baron Sojin," she said crisply. "It was bad enough to be kidnapped, but I don't relish being awakened in the middle of the night!"

"I'm sorry, Diana," said the Baron soothingly, indicating a chair. "This is urgent, and could not wait until morning."

Diana sat in the chair and watched the Baron intently. She looked as fresh as though it were mid-day and not the middle of the night.

"I'm waiting," she said impatiently.

"I have a few questions to ask Diana," replied Sojin, going back to his desk. "Questions that cannot wait until morning."

"Very well, then," the girl retorted. "Ask them."

"You must tell me all you know about The Phantom," said Sojin.

For once his control had deserted him. He struck his clenched fist on the desk. The heavy walnut fixture shivered with the impact. Diana stared wide-eyed.

"I've nothing to say," she said through tight lips.

Baron Sojin stepped toward her, his eyes blazing. Instinctively, Diana shrank back, thinking that he was going to strike her. The sudden ringing of the telephone stopped him in his tracks.

Sojin's face changed. The film cleared from his eyes. He smiled his sinister smile.

"Forgive me, my dear," he murmured.

He picked up the phone.

"This is the radio room, sir," came Colonel Crang's voice. "I'm sorry to bother you at this hour, but something important has happened."

"That's quite all right, Colonel," said Sojin, smoothly.

He was master of himself now and he glanced at Diana reassuringly.

"I'm always at Scorpia's disposal."

Diana walked over toward the table and watched the Baron's face closely as the conversation continued.

"I just received a transmission from Westchester," said the Colonel.

"Something seems to be seriously wrong there."

"What do you mean, Colonel?" Sojin snapped. His knuckles tightened on the receiver.

"The agent acted with admirable initiative," Crang went on. "He was about to report in to Otto Koch when he saw a police car stop in front of the farmhouse he is using as headquarters. He hid and watched. He witnessed the arrest of our entire staff, including Koch. He immediately used his emergency transmitter and called us. Can you hear me, sir?"

"I hear you, Colonel," said Sojin. His face was grimly set.

"That means that the last messages from Westchester were not genuine, Baron," Crang went on urgently. "The police are monitoring all our calls—probably using Cringle under duress—while at the same time, sending us false messages reporting everything normal."

"The significance of this had not entirely escaped me, Colonel," replied Sojin, keeping his brilliant blue eyes fixed on Diana. "We had a message from someone called The Phantom earlier. Tell our operators to find out everything they can about him and report any information, immediately."

He paused a moment.

"And Colonel Crang, I suppose we have checked the authenticity of this latest message?"

He listened intently.

"Very well, Colonel. That is good. Keep an international alert."

He concentrated intently for a minute or two. Diana could almost sense the impatience of Colonel Crang waiting in the radio room. Sojin finally made up his mind.

"Three orders, Colonel. No more radio contact with Westchester. We will accept no messages from them. Secondly, double the guard on the island, day and night. Anything that moves is to be shot! And thirdly, Colonel Crang, join me here in my quarters as soon as you have carried out my orders."

"Very good, sir."

There was a click as Crang put down the phone. Baron Sojin turned back to Diana.

"And, now, my dear, it is time you and I had a serious chat about your friend, The Phantom."

CHAPTER 23

Strange Calling Card

The Phantom slipped cautiously out of his parachute harness and dropped gently to the ground. The harness remained swaying in the darkness, suspended from a branch, ten feet up. The big man could not dislodge it, but he felt certain no one would discover it before morning. And by morning, he hoped to have accomplished his mission. He slipped between the trees like a shadow, making for the dark bulk of the castle, silver-etched in the moonlight, about a quarter of a mile away.

He moved silently and stealthily, with all the accumulated jungle instincts of his ancestors. Only a few sleepy animals saw him pass and then they again settled down for the night. Presently, The Phantom came to the edge of a steep escarpment. Far below, the ocean dashed whitely against its base. He emerged from the edge of the jungle and walked over jagged, rocky outcrops. It was a brilliant night and he could see a long way ahead.

Nothing moved in the wilderness of stone, but he kept in the shadows and with infinite caution made his way up the cliff-face until he was within ten feet of the top. Here he paused to get his bearings. All he could see of the castle now was its top-most turrets. Tiny squares of yellow light showed from this quarter. So someone was awake. Perhaps the higher echelons of Scorpia, worried at the message he had sent them? The Phantom grinned to himself in the darkness. Well, they would soon have something more tangible to worry them.

He moved on, scaling the last few feet, until he put his strong, steel-like fingers over the edge of the plateau. Inch by inch the big man lifted himself until his eyes were at ground level. He found he could see several hundred yards. The place was worn smooth and level with the passage of thousands of pairs of boots over the years. From the stone blocks, the saluting base and other military detail, The Phantom deduced that it was nothing less than a gigantic parade ground. And there, not ten yards away from him, was a big man in a military uniform, armed with a sub-machine gun. The Phantom smiled grimly as he ducked down out of sight

The sentry continued his pacing. He walked along the edge of the plateau until he was no more than a yard from where The Phantom crouched. The bright flare of a match came from above as the man lit a cigarette. The Phantom moved behind him. The soldier was just talking the cigarette from his mouth when his ankles were seized in a grip like steel. Before he could react, he was lifted completely from the ground. He screamed once, and then his head was dashed against the surface of the parade ground with stunning force. He rolled over limply as the slap of heavy boots sounded from farther up.

A second sentry ran into sight, his feet echoing from the cliff-side. He brought his sub-machine gun up with a gasp as he saw the sprawled figure of his companion.

"What's the matter?" he called nervously. "Did you fall?"

The other man made no reply. The second sentry came up to him and rolled him over cautiously. Then, he recoiled, looking carefully about him. Stamped into the side of the man's jaw was the mark of a skull which seemed to have been imprinted into the flesh. The sentry's jaw sagged.

"The mark of a skull!" he gasped. "What does that mean?"

"Just this!" said a powerful, resonant voice from behind him. As the sentry jumped back, a mighty force plucked the sub-machine gun from his hands. He was whirled like a toy doll by a force he was unable to comprehend. He saw a square, strong face with a black mask over the eyes before he was dashed to the ground like his companion, and consciousness left him.

The Phantom bent swiftly over the second sentry.

"This is more like it," he told himself. "The Phantom strikes like a thunderbolt but moves softer than a stalking tiger" –old jungle saying!

As he moved away into the shadows, hard up against the Castle wall, there came the sound of more running footsteps. Torches flickered as a squad of soldiers poured from the open gates of the keep, fanning out across the parade ground. The Phantom continued to move along the wall, then slipped within the Castle walls. Only an animal with its senses hyper-tuned to the ways of the wild could have detected him, so swiftly did he move. In the deeper shadow of the inner courtyard, The

Phantom hugged the wall and glided silently along.

Colonel Crang's massive face bisected by his thick, black mustache looked as impassive as ever as he reported to the Baron. Sojin stood erect in his dressing gown and looked from the correct figure of the soldier in his immaculate uniform to the slight figure of Diana Palmer in her nightclothes in the chair.

"This is a serious situation, Colonel," he told the Chief of his Security Forces.

"I acknowledge that, sir, which was why I hastened to warn you," said Crang with a short inclination of his head toward his master.

He looked grimly at the girl.

"If you will permit me to make an observation, sir, this circumstance might never have arisen if you had taken my advice in the first place."

Sojin's blue eyes turned piercingly upon the Colonel. His slim body quivered and he took one step forward. Dark blood suffused his cheeks. But his voice was soft and low as he replied.

"You are not permitted to make observations, Colonel Crang. Your remarks are impertinent and out of order. Under less grave circumstances, I would have no hesitation in taking a disciplinary action."

He paused and Colonel Crang turned pale.

He made a stiff bow toward the Baron and said in clipped tones, "Believe me, sir, I had only the security of Scorpia at heart when I made my suggestion."

"Very well then, Crang," said the Baron moodily, his anger past. "I'll accept that. We'll say no more about it."

He turned to Diana Palmer who sat quietly in her chair, taking no part in the heated discussion.

"This Phantom of yours led the police to our Westchester center of operations. I've had enough double-talk from you. Who is he?"

All the gentleness and chivalry had gone from his manner now. He spoke harshly and the thin, bleached slit of his mouth made an ugly line across his face.

Diana smiled.

"You read about him in your history of Scorpia, Baron," she said. "Don't you remember? He is The Ghost Who Walks, the man who cannot die. . ."

"Enough of this foolery!" Crang interrupted. "Give us information about him, or you might not like the consequences."

He put his hand significantly to his belt.

"Scorpia has long experience in making people talk, my girl," Sojin told Diana in a controlled voice." "Now, tell me everything you know about this person or I'll. . ."

He stopped, aware that the door had opened unceremoniously

and that a tottering figure was framed there.

"What is it?" he asked the valet irritably.

"Don't you know after all these years that you should never enter my apartment without permission, much less without knocking?"

"Your pardon, Excellency!" the man stammered. "The circumstances are unprecedented."

"Spit it out, man!" said Crang impatiently.

"If you please, sir," said the valet, looking at his master with a trembling visage.

"The Phantom is here!"

CHAPTER 24

Unexpected Visitor

There was a moment of stunned silence. Diana was on her feet, her face suffused with happiness. Crang looked unbelievingly at the valet while Baron Sojin stood as though turned to stone. Crang was the first to recover himself.

"What do you mean, The Phantom is here, you fool?" he said harshly.

The servant screamed with pain as the Colonel jumped forward and seized him by the wrist.

"Please, sir," he howled. "I only meant that The Phantom has arrived on Scorpia. He knocked out two men on the parade ground."

"Old fool!" Crang growled, as he let go of the man's arm. He turned back to the Baron.

"I'd better investigate."

"I'll go with you," said Baron Sojin.

"You stay here!" he told Diana. He led the way out of the room, the valet almost unable to keep up. The three were hardly able to cram into the private elevator that shot them swiftly to the lower levels of the castle. Already the garrison had been alerted, and soldiers and officers were clattering up and down the stairs. Powerful floodlights swept the courtyard and the Castle walls. The ranks parted as the Baron and Crang hurried across to the small group clustered around two men lying on the ground.

"Let us through," said Crang impatiently.

He recognized one of the saluting officers.

"Ah, Carson, I assume you are off duty from the radio room?"

"Yes, sir," said Carson saluting briskly.

"Well, take charge here," said Crang, looking around him. "There has been enough panic for one evening."

He knelt by the Baron, who was examining the recumbent men. The valet was at his side. He gulped as he looked at the soldiers' faces.

"You see, Excellency," he said pointing to the vivid blotches stamped in their flesh. "There is the skull mark. The sign of the Skull is the mark of The Phantom, sir. It has been so down through all the ages!"

"Nonsense!" snapped Sojin but, nevertheless, he felt a constriction in his throat.

He looked furtively round him, reassured by the presence of the soldiers and their weapons.

"We'd better get these men inside, close the gates and double the sentries," Crang said.

"See to it. Colonel," Sojin said shortly, getting to his feet. "Then rejoin me in the Armory."

"The Armory, sir?" said Crang, looking puzzled.

"You heard me, Colonel," Sojin replied.

He lingered.

"We are surrounded by a thousand miles of ocean. How could anyone get here?"

Colonel Crang shrugged.

"I heard an aircraft passing over earlier tonight, sir. Someone may have parachuted down."

The Baron looked at him keenly. He seemed to have somewhat recovered himself now.

"Well-deduced, Colonel," he said. "That is a possibility."

"I'll have a search made for parachutes, sir," said Crang. "They may have dropped more than one man."

He started issuing instructions to the troops as the Baron went swiftly back inside the courtyard. Before his eyes was the livid emblem of the skull.

"I'll get at the truth," he told himself, as the elevator carried him effortlessly upwards.

Diana's face blanched as she saw the expression on the Baron's face. He rushed up to the gallery and came back with a book. He seized her by the arm and dragged her down a flight of stairs. They entered through a massive, iron-bound door, which the Baron left open behind them. The chamber inside was a big one, but not as large as the Baron's own private room.

The walls were of stone and a gallery ran around three sides. There were racks of weapons along the walls and on the gallery; animal heads and other trophies, suits of armour, cutlasses, every conceivable type of weapon, old and new. Large, carved chests stood about the floor and an alcove at one end was covered by thick curtains. The Baron prowled about for a few minutes, visibly nervous. He went to look behind the curtains and even up the balcony.

Then he went to stand by a telephone on a big, oak table and looked at Diana with his strange blue eyes.

"This is my Armory," he said. "There are no windows in this room and only two doors, one of them bolted. When Colonel Crang joins us and the second door is barred, no one—not even The Phantom—will be able to get in."

There was contempt in Diana's eyes as she looked at the ruler of Scorpia.

"You're such a brave pirate!" she said in scornful tones. "Afraid of a ghost? You locked yourself in a room without windows."

The Baron had raised his arm to strike her when there was a clatter of boots on the stairs. Colonel Crang was at the door. He saluted, slamming and bolting the big iron- bound door behind him.

"Your orders have been carried out, sir. My men are searching the island."

"Excellent, Colonel," said Baron Sojin. "You are just in time. I was about to question Miss Palmer more intently."

The Colonel put his hand to a coiled whip at his belt "Perhaps you would permit me, sir?"

The Baron shook his head.

"Maybe there was something in what you said after all. This is a pleasure I reserve for myself."

He faced Diana squarely and looked at her with his piercing, blue eyes. His lips twisted in a strange smile as he observed, "I am hereditary King of Scorpia! People obey my commands or die! Tell me who The Phantom is or you won't leave this room alive."

The girl remained silent for a moment. Sojin, conscious that he had been speaking a great deal during the last hour, felt a dryness in his throat. He reached across the table and picked up a crystal beaker. He poured himself a measure of white wine into a long-sternmed glass. As he raised it to his lips he glanced at the rim of the glass. His hand trembled involuntarily. There, stamped into the surface of the vessel, was that terrible symbol of the skull. Sojin staggered and the glass shattered on the floor of the room. The Baron gazed wildly at the puzzled face of Crang.

"It's The Phantom!" the ruler of Scorpia gasped. "He's been in this room."

He ran quickly to the door to examine the fastenings. His breath caught in his throat and his heart started thumping faster when he saw another skull symbol, this time imprinted on the handle of the door.

He turned back to Crang, who looked around him apprehensively.

"I can't understand it," gasped Sojin, feeling as though he were in a trap instead of the comforting protection of the Armory.

"It's perfectly simple, King of Scorpia!" said a strong, mocking voice behind him.

CHAPTER 25

Sabre Showdown

Sojin stood as though turned to bronze. Colonel Crang's jaw fell open, his hand stopped halfway to the whip at his belt. Diana's eyes filled with tears of grateful thanks. All stared incredulously at the tall form of The Phantom which had apparently sprung from nowhere. His muscular body rippled with strength as he jumped lightly from a great oak chest which stood against the wall of the armory. From beneath the lid peeped the trembling visage of old Miki, the handyman.

He stood up awkwardly, and bowed feebly in the Baron's direction.

"Surrender, Excellency!" he said in quavering tones. "This is The Phantom. He is the Ghost Who Walks, the one who never dies!"

"You old fool!" snarled Colonel Crang. His hand came up with his revolver, making a blurred arc in the light of the overhead lamps.

The Phantom whirled with one lithe movement. The surprised face of Crang turned upside down as he seized his gun-arm, and the enormously bulky figure of the Chief of Security went cart wheeling through the air. He came down with shattering force on the table, smashing the candelabra and sending pewterware flying. The gun skidded harmlessly across the tiles.

Baron Sojin staggered back against the Armory door as Diana ran across the floor. Then she was in Kit's arms, with his strong fingers caressing her cheek.

"Diana," he whispered over and over again. "I knew you weren't dead."

"Darling, Kit," said Diana. "If you only knew how glad I am to see you."

Old Miki shouted as a sword whistled through the air and splintered a stool behind them.

"We'll continue this in a minute," said The Phantom, grinning.

Sojin tore free and gained the balcony, hearing The Phantom's feet pounding up the gallery staircase behind him. He went for a big rack of sabres at the near end. He whirled, the steel slicing through the air.

"Let's see how you like pirate steel, O One Who Never Dies!" he shouted sarcastically.

His triumphant cry turned to a howl of pain as a rack of muskets, torn from the wall by the Phantom's steel-strong hands, slid along the floor and cracked against his shins. Then The Phantom jumped to the sabres. His teeth flashed beneath the black mask as he wheeled. The blade in his hand made a dazzling shimmer in the lamp-light

"I like cold steel very well, Your Excellency!" he laughed. "You see, I was educated in the United States. And it was there I mastered the use of the sabre!"

Diana heard the clash of steel from the balcony above as Colonel Crang got up heavily. There was a dazed look in his eyes.

He howled with pain as the girl cracked him with the shaft of a pike she snatched from the wall. He crashed to the floor.

The Phantom swerved gracefully as Sojin's sabre cut splinters from a priceless carved table at his elbow. Perspiration was running down the Baron's face, but he was a fine swordsman and there was plenty of fight left in him.

"Why don't you give up, Excellency?" said The Phantom, jumping up on top of an oak bench and effortlessly parrying the other's thrust The clash of the steel had an exhilarating effect on him, and, as the Baron redoubled his efforts, it seemed only to increase his energy.

"Why don't you stand still?" Sojin snapped irritably, the perspiration staining his pajamas. He had thrown aside his robe when the fight began, but he was puzzled at the brilliant technique of this peculiar swordsman, and already the jacket of his pajamas, where it billowed out, was slashed in two places.

"There are no rules in your sort of fighting, Baron," said The Phantom, jumping down from the bench and parrying his way along the edge of the balcony. He waved encouragingly to Diana. He saw that Crang was now on the floor with an oak bench on top of him and Diana on top of the bench. He grinned.

Sojin came at him in a mad rush then, forcing him to the edge of the railing. The Phantom stood on the rail, jumped outwards as the sabre blade whistled viciously beneath his boots, reaching the chandelier on its heavy supporting chains. He stood supporting himself by the central chain, making a great arc through the air. His blade splintered the balcony near

Sojin and the Baron sprang back. He was spluttering incoherently with rage.

"Why don't you stand still?" he screamed.

"Certainly, Baron," said The Phantom. He wrenched the chandelier chain and came forward in another great arching swoop. He let go and in a tremendous leap through space cleared the balcony and was at the Baron's throat before the ruler of Scorpia knew what had happened. He fell backwards over a table, all the breath knocked out of him. Steel clashed for the last time as The Phantom pinned his sword-arm. Sojin found a sharp blade pricking his throat.

"I really think it's time you surrendered," The Phantom said.

Baron Sojin sat sullenly at the telephone in the Armory. Colonel Crang's head was being bound up by Miki, who had a secret smile of glee on his face. The Phantom leaned on his sabre, Diana at his side, and surveyed the scene of wreckage that had once been an elegant room.

"Places without windows have their disadvantages, Baron!" he told Sojin lightly.

"Now just tell your men to stack their arms in the courtyard and assemble in the dungeons."

He turned back to the old handyman and waited until the Baron had picked up the telephone and given his instructions. "When that's done," he told Miki, "go down and lock them all in and bring me back the keys."

The old man bowed.

"It shall be done, O Ghost Who Walks!" he said.

He was about to scuttle off when the big man called him back.

"All except Lieutenant Carson," he said. "We shall need him. Tell him to go to the radio room and wait."

The old man left and The Phantom drew Diana close to his side. He looked coolly at Baron Sojin and the sullen figure of Colonel Crang.

"Accept defeat with grace," he advised them. "All good things have to come to an end, but, after all, Scorpia lasted for over four hundred years!"

A scowl was the only reply from Sojin.

"Now," said The Phantom going across to lean over him. "The American 7th Fleet is on battle exercises only about six hours steaming time from here. We passed them in the plane on our way over. I want you to send them a message. And here's what you're to say."

He gave his instructions to Sojin and a few minutes later there came a knock at the door. Miki was back with the keys.

"All locked in, O Ghost Who Never Dies!" he said with satisfaction, basking in the smiles Diana and the big man gave him.

"When you've finished those chores, I want you to get radio contact with Westchester," The Phantom ordered Sojin. He gave Diana an affectionate squeeze.

"It's about time your mother and your uncle heard your voice again."

It was near dawn before the sound of sirens and the beat of powerful motors reached the group in the Armory. Leaving Diana with a gun trained on Sojin and Crang, The Phantom went out onto the terrace. Two powerful cruisers and a destroyer had dropped anchor off the island. Fast launches were already speeding ashore, loaded to the gunwales with Marines.

The Phantom laughed as heavy-booted feet echoed on the staircases of Castle Toeplitz. He hurried back to the Armory.

"The Marines have landed and the situation is well in hand," he told Sojin.

Before he could reply the door burst open and the room was full of steel-helmeted bluejackets.

A broad-shouldered man with a bristling mustache was at The Phantom's elbow. He stared at the big man.

"I'm Colonel Robbins," he announced. "What's going on here?"

"Too long a story to tell you now," said The Phantom. "Just lock those two up. You'll find several hundred more in the dungeons."

He shook the Colonel by the hand.

"This is Miss Diana Palmer, who was lost at sea a few days ago."

He chuckled at the Marine Colonel's expression.

"What does this all mean?" said the latter.

"It means that a four-hundred-year-old Empire of Evil called the Scorpia has been broken," said The Phantom. He took Diana by the arm and they went out onto the battlements, oblivious to the noise of men's feet tramping up and down stone corridors.

The Phantom looked at Diana as she gazed down at the blue sea and the grey steel outlines of the warships.

"It's difficult to believe, Kit," whispered Diana, "that we're here together like this."

"And it's all thanks to you," said the big man.

"What do you mean, Kit?" replied the girl.

"You smashed Scorpia, darling," her companion said. "If it hadn't been for your research none of this would have happened."

She lifted her head and placed her hands on each side of The Phantom's face as though she were memorizing every line.

She stopped at the sound of a cough behind her. A young Marine Lieutenant stood there with a pink, embarrassed face.

"Radio telephone contact with Westchester, Miss Palmer," he said. "Your mother is waiting to speak to you."

Diana's face was alight with happiness.

"I'll be back soon, darling," she said, "to take up where we left off."

The Phantom turned back to the battlements, the sun hot and dazzling on his face, as the sound of Diana's footsteps died away down the Castle stairway.

"We most certainly will," he said.

COMING SOON FROM HERMES PRESS

Volume 4: The Veiled Lady!